The Grove
& Other Stories

EZRA T. GRAY

Printed in the United States of America

First Edition: August 1, 2012
Second Edition: August 1, 2014

ISBN: 0990581802
ISBN-13: 978-0990581802

Johntown Crier Press LLC
P.O Box 1174
Marion, MT 59925

www.JohntownCrierPress.com

CONTENTS

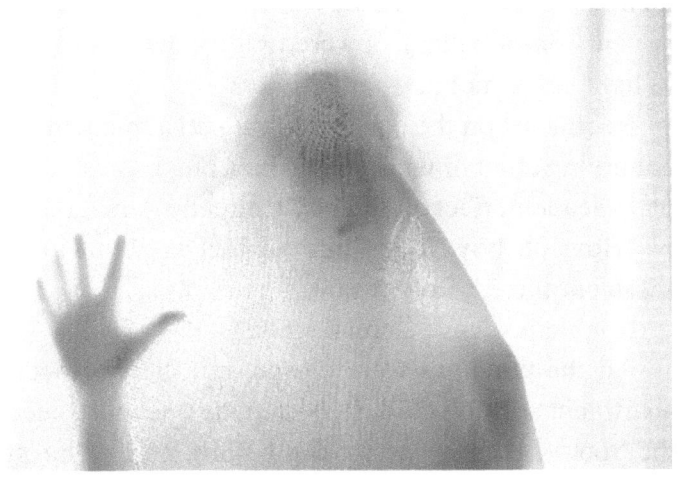

THE NEIGHBORHOOD'S GONE TO HELL

Stillness lay across the city like a thick wet blanket, and an unnatural chill permeated the motionless night air. Thick, ominous clouds boiled over the western horizon, and a blood red moon obscured the stars just above them.

With a shiver, Robert secured the window and pulled the curtain closed. A candle flickered on the coffee table causing shadows to move across the walls. Shadows moved in other places in the apartment as well, though

Robert had lived with them for so long he no longer saw them. A soft Barry Manilow hit from the late seventies issued from a battery-powered radio, but it did nothing to lighten the mood.

Robbie sat on the couch, looking up at his father. The unnerving quiet of what should be a bustling fall evening had a leaden effect on the boy's already damaged spirit.

"Boy, oh boy, looks like all hell is about to break loose out there," Robert said.

Robbie just gave a small smile.

All the windows were closed, but the two-bedroom apartment still felt cold. Robert made one more check of the rooms then went to the bathroom. As he stood urinating a cold shudder ran down his spine. The candle on the sink flickered, casting an eldritch image of himself on the wall beside him. He quickly finished his business and washed his hands. "Well," he mused, "at least the water is still on."

On the way back to the living room, Robert stopped to retrieve a quilt from his bed. As he turned to go, Sue moved. His breath caught and every pore tingled to life before he could tell himself it was the candlelight that made it seem as though the picture had moved. Sadness filled him, threatened to overwhelm him, and he sat down on the edge of the bed, every muscle tensed against the crushing weight of her memory.

The very bed he sat on held the strongest memories. He and Sue had purchased it at a secondhand shop when they were first married. They refinished it. They used it.

They made a baby on it. The baby, now nine, had been brought home from the hospital and laid on it. It amazed him how much of his life centered around the bed. He couldn't part with it and still slept on it, though not alone. Although Robbie had a fine bed of his own, since his mother went away, he clung to his father like a lifeline.

Sue's body was never found, but the rescuers assured him she was gone. The call had come in on a night much like this one. Sir, we regret to inform you… There were no survivors… He could hear the sadness in the caller's voice and feel the clenching pain in his chest as though it were happening now instead of last year. Her plane had just disappeared, blown up in midair, taking his sweet love with it.

Sue hated to fly and almost never did. But she was so practical, and there were times when she just couldn't avoid it. She had even bought that special insurance at the last minute at the ticket counter. It was ironic. Together, he and Sue had always struggled financially. Now he had plenty of money, but no Sue.

At least he could afford to stay home with Robbie. They had no one else for comfort. Both of his parents were killed in a fire the year after he and Sue married. He had uncles and aunts and cousins, but they all lived far away, and he was not close to any of them. He and Robbie walked alone.

Robert shook himself, took a deep breath and, with a practiced effort, pulled himself back from the brink. It would do Robbie no good to see him beaten down like this.

In the living room, Robert smiled at Robbie. "Hey, kid, you cold?" Robbie nodded. "Well, I'm glad it's not just me. I thought I was coming down with something." At Robbie's worried look, Robert hastened to add, "don't worry, I'm not going anywhere."

Since Sue died, Robbie had become obsessive about his father's well being. Robert understood this fear, the fear that he would be abandoned by his father as he'd been abandoned by his mother. It was not her fault, but Robert, too, felt abandoned, feelings for which he carried much guilt.

"Want to share the quilt?" he asked, as he plopped down next to his son. He flung the quilt across them, then stretched out on the couch, pushing his feet behind Robbie's back.

"Dad, your shoes are still on!"

"Scoot up this way."

After Robbie snuggled up against him, Robert situated the blanket over them and they lay quietly, listening to the radio and watching the flickering of the candle.

Outside, the night was still calm. The black monsters in the sky crept closer. Lightning flickered brightly. If Robert had been at the window, he would have seen, if for only a brief second, a sinister face in the clouds, a giant outline of Man's nemesis with a wicked grin on its gothic features.

Curled up on the couch, Robert, of course, saw none of this, but he felt it. Even under the blanket, with the combined warmth of their bodies, the two were cold. An evil was creeping up on them, and no amount of cuddling would make it go away.

Freddie Fender was just beginning 'Before the Next Teardrop Falls,' when the couch started to shake. Robert had only been in one, but he knew instantly this was an earthquake. He tried to rise, but the violent movement of the couch prevented him from doing so. Terrified that the upstairs apartment might come crashing down on them, he clutched Robbie close, hoping his body would protect the boy.

Then, just as suddenly as it began, the quake was over. Robert jumped up from the couch and ran to the window, fearing the worst. The candle on the table remained upright, but Freddie's tinny voice was muffled by the carpet where the radio had fallen. As Robert pulled the curtain aside, a wisp of white swept past the window. "What was that?" he muttered. The movement wasn't repeated and he dismissed it as a trick of the night.

The clouds had descended upon the city, and the air was no longer calm. Leaves and debris swirled across the yard on a stiff breeze, but all the buildings he could see appeared to be intact.

"Dad? What was that? Was it a quake?"

Robert looked down at Robbie's pale face. "Yes, it was a quake. We studied about them in your Geology book, remember?"

Freddie's song went quiet in mid-sentence, leaving the two staring at one another in deafening silence.

Robert tried to sound calm. "Guess the station went out."

"Dad, I'm scared."

"Oh, son, no worries. The quake probably shook something loose."

He looked out the window again. The wind had picked up. White things were swirling in a gale-force wind. "What the hell?" Robert strained to see what the wind had picked up. Perhaps a neighbor's laundry was being blown about. The red moon was gone, tucked behind the spongy blackness of the thunderheads. A white swirl fluttered again. It's probably a bed sheet blown from somebody's clothesline, he thought.

He started to pull the curtain but stopped as the sheet swirled closer. It wafted toward Robert until it hung vertically, edges rippling gently, about a foot off the ground.

"What in the—"

Just as Robert started to speak, the sheet turned and flew straight at the window. As Robert's eyes widened in shock, it took on a luminous glow, and he gasped as he realized it was no sheet. The specter closed in on him, forming a beautiful angelic face with long glowing streamers flowing behind. Then, just as suddenly, the face changed into a hideous skull with hollow black eye sockets and decaying broken teeth. A mournful wail erupted from the grotesque apparition, now just inches from Robert's face. He screamed and flung himself backward, flipping over the couch and knocking the candle off the coffee table.

Robbie was up in a flash, retrieving the candle. "Dad! Daddy, what's wrong?"

"Ah, I...something is out there! I, ah—" Robert was cut short by another wail followed by a very human scream. The next sound they heard was a sickening thud right outside the window. Robert got up. He knew he had to look. He didn't want to, but he knew he must. He lifted the edge of the curtain. Even in the near pitch black, he could see the body of Mr. Bailey, their upstairs neighbor. On the lawn, the single apparition had been joined by several others. The luminous ghouls swirled around Mr. Bailey's body like a phantasmagorical windmill.

"Daddy!" Robbie whispered. Robert realized the boy had crept up beside him. "Daddy, what are those things?"

"I don't know, son."

"Daddy, are they ghosts?" Robert didn't reply, he just watched the unbelievable scene playing out a few feet away. "Dad, are they, huh?"

"I-I-I don't know what the hell they are, but I'll tell you this, son, I'm scared as hell!" The wind howled louder, whistling around the edges of the window sill. Robert looked up into the night sky. There were hundreds of phantoms floating to and fro. "Oh, dear God, what is happening?" He could hear other screams, and other moans.

It was all he could stand. Robert jerked the curtain down and fell into the corner, pulling Robbie to his chest as he did so. With a trembling hand he pulled the quilt from the couch and wrapped it around them, covering the boy's head.

"Our Father, who art in Heaven, hallowed be thy name—" Robert's prayer was shattered by a pounding at the door. He didn't know who or what was there, but he was certain it wasn't anyone he wanted to see. The pounding continued. Robert squeezed Robbie tighter and continued to pray. The wind roared like a freight train and rattled the window in its frame, but the pounding rose above it all. Robbie pressed his hands over his ears and closed his eyes tight as though he could shut everything out with the sheer force of his will. The pounding took on a desperate rhythm, and Robert could take it no more.

He rose from the corner, reeling like a drunken sailor, and staggered towards the door. What monstrous fiend awaited him, he knew not, but something deep within him drove him on. He forced his eye against the peephole. It was a woman.

"Please!" He could hear her pleading. "Please, dear Lord, help me!" Robert fumbled with the chain.

"Daddy, don't!" Robbie yelled. "Don't do it!" But it was too late. Robert had pulled the door open.

The outside world was not the same world that had greeted Robert each time he'd opened the door for the past ten years. The sky was clouded, but no longer dark.

Alien clouds glowed red and churned as though stirred by a giant hand. Robert gasped. Thousands of ghouls swirled about just above the trees and houses.

To his right, Mr. Bailey's body had been raised upright by several of the wraiths. They swirled around the elderly man in a horrifying dance, then one of them forced his mouth open. They forced it too far, and Robert could hear bones cracking. Suddenly one of the things slithered into the opening and disappeared. The acrid taste of bile rose in the back of Robert's throat as Mr. Bailey's body jerked and came to life. The reanimated corpse tottered about the small yard for a moment then lurched away down the sidewalk and around the corner of the building.

"Hey, wasn't that Mr. Bailey? From upstairs?"

Robert started, the macabre show having distracted him from the reason he opened the door in the first place. "I...well...I think it used to be."

"Well, thank God you opened the door. I thought you would never let me in!"

"Well...uh, who are you?" He looked over at her. Her eyes reminded him of Sue's, soft and kind.

I'm Sharon, your neighbor. You know, next door?" She gestured down the wall at another door, identical to Robert's.

Robert remembered the landlord telling him there would be a new tenant, but he hadn't seen anyone actually move in. "Oh, well, uh—" Suddenly one of the wraiths swirled in uncomfortably close to them. Robert grabbed the woman by the arm and yanked her inside, slamming the door and throwing the deadbolt with his other hand. He slid the chain lock on then sagged against the door in relief.

Robbie came over and eyed their newcomer curiously. "What is happening out there?"

"Hell," Sharon answered. "Hell has come to earth. This is the beginning of the end."

"It's what?" Robert asked. "You mean, like, pitchfork-wielding devils and all that stuff?" He shook his head in disbelief.

"Hell," she said, patiently, "is not a place, it's a who."

"A who?"

"Revelations, chapter six, verse eight. 'And I looked and behold a pale horse, and his name that sat on him was Death, and Hell followed with him.'"

"Ah…well, yes, of course." The truth was, Robert hadn't darkened the door of a church since Sue's death.

"Anyway, it has started. The two worlds have collided and become one."

"But I never thought it would be this way. I mean, my wife, she—"

"Oh! Is she out there? You must be very worried."

Robert shook his head. "I'm a widower." The words sounded strange coming from his mouth. It was, he realized, the first time he'd ever said it.

Sharon smiled kindly. "I'm sorry."

"No, it's okay. She's been gone nearly a year, now."

"You must have loved her very much."

"Yes, yes," Robert replied, "yes, I did. I do…I…"

Sharon stepped closer to Robert and pushed her finger to his lips. "It's okay," she whispered, "I understand."

At her touch, Robert's heart skipped a beat. He could feel the essence of the woman near him. He had thought he would be uncomfortable, being this close to a woman other than Sue, but he was not. In fact, he was at ease, more at ease than he'd been at any time in the last year. As he looked into her soft brown eyes, with their warmth so like his beloved Sue's, he almost felt guilty. The spell was broken when Robbie spoke.

"Dad? Ahem, earth to Dad?"

"Oh, ah, Sharon, this is my son Robbie. Robert Junior."

"It's nice to meet you, young man." Sharon held out her hand, and Robbie shook it. "You are a fine looking lad," she said.

Robbie smiled shyly at her. "Thank you, ma'am."

"Back to what we were talking about," Robert said. "You really think this is the end, I mean, Armageddon and all?"

"I don't think, I know."

"But how do you know?"

Sharon suddenly looked uneasy. "I, well, I've studied this sort of thing."

"Well, for the sake of argument, let's say you're right. What do we do?"

"Nothing," she replied. "We wait."

"Wait? Wait for what?"

"There is a seven-year period to the tribulation. A lot has to happen between now and then."

"You know I never imagined it would be like this."

Sharon gave a little laugh. "Lots of things are not like we imagined."

"Look, I'm sorry, would you like a cup of coffee or something?"

"No, no, I'm fine, but I would like to sit down."

"Please," Robert gestured toward the couch, embarrassed, "have a seat."

The flickering of the candle cast a soft glow throughout the room, which seemed a little brighter for Sharon's presence. Except for the fact that the outside world had turned upside down, the scene in the tiny apartment's front room could have been that of any normal home. But it was not. Of course it was not.

Sharon sat on the couch and Robert in a chair nearby. Robbie bent down in the corner to retrieve the quilt, and the window above him exploded inward. A hand reached through the glass and grabbed the collar of his shirt. It was Mr. Bailey's hand. Before Robert could rise from the chair, Robbie had been dragged through the window and was gone.

"Robbie!" Sharon screamed.

For a split second, all movement stopped. Then, in slow motion, Robert sprang from his chair and ran ponderously to the door. He dragged the deadbolt open and laboriously slid off the chain. As the door creaked open, time caught up with an obscene slap.

Standing on the threshold were two visitors Robert hadn't seen in years. When the door swung open wide, Robert came face to face with the charred corpses of his mom and dad. Once again he could feel the acid rise in the back of his throat, but this time he couldn't hold it back.

Fortunately for Robert, he had eaten a light lunch. What came up was mostly bile and then dry heaves.

With all his heart, Robert believed that his mom and dad had gone to be with Jesus. The things standing on the threshold were not truly his parents any more than a shoe is truly a foot. At death, the body is shed like clothing at the end of the day. But Robert had come to recognize these bodies as his mom and dad, and now he desperately wanted to go hide under his bed. Of course, he couldn't—Robbie was out there.

But to get out there he had to get past his dead parents.

Only a few seconds had passed since Robbie was grabbed, but to Robert, it seemed like a lifetime. He took a deep breath, bracing himself to push past them. Then his mother raised her arm. The hand that had cared for and nurtured Robert throughout his life was now a blackened stub with bits of bone poking out the end. Her lips parted, as though to speak, but instead of words, maggots poured out. Robert shrank back, and his mouth drew down in horror as the larvae hit the ground. He would have vomited again, but just then Robbie gave an anguished cry.

The sound snapped Robert back from his nightmare. He darted forward, intending to try to slip past his dear parents, but as he cleared the door, the toe of his shoe hung on the raised threshold, and his left shoulder came in contact with his mother's face. He cringed, but instead of hearing bone popping and feeling rotting flesh, he heard the flutter of wings and felt those wings brushing his face. The two corpses disintegrated into dozens of common, garden variety wrens.

Robert slapped them away from his face and staggered out into the yard. Above him, the sky was a brighter red. The crimson clouds churned violently, now less than a hundred feet from the ground. The very air glowed. Zombie-like beings, victims of bodily takeovers like Mr. Bailey, meandered down the street and along the sidewalks. Wraiths swirled about, and the neighborhood now looked much like Hell on Earth.

Mr. Bailey's reanimated corpse was dragging Robbie, kicking and screaming, across the yard by the collar of his shirt. As he ran toward them, Robert saw Robbie's aluminum bat lying in the grass. He had scolded the boy many times for leaving it out, but now he was glad for the child's negligence. He scooped it up and hefted it in his right hand as he ran.

Robert had never considered himself a powerful man, but he was past scared. He was past horrified and into a realm of terror few humans ever reach. He swung the bat for all he was worth. The club made contact with old Mr. Bailey's head. The body jerked around and then stiffened as the old gentleman's cranium rolled past the sidewalk and into the gutter. The body released its grip on Robbie, took several steps, spinning in a circle as it did, then collapsed on the grass.

Curiously, Robert saw, there was no blood. What did flow from the mangled mess that had been Mr. Bailey's neck, was white, almost transparent. As the last of it trickled out, the body gave a final shudder. After a second the wraith gathered itself up and swirled away. Only then did blood flow from Mr. Bailey's neck, running down the sidewalk and into the gutter, pooling around his severed head.

Robert didn't wait to see what would happen next. He grabbed Robbie and ran back to the apartment. Sharon was waiting just outside the door.

"Oh my gosh, Robert. You knocked his head right off! I've never seen anything like it!"

Robert didn't stop to talk, pulling Sharon inside with him as he ran through the door. With Robbie still tucked under his arm, he slammed the door and re-secured the locks. Only then did he set the boy down so he could look at the broken window. Robert knew it would only be a matter of time before another corpse discovered them.

While Sharon held Robbie on the couch, smoothing his hair and fussing over him, Robert ran to the utility room where he had some plywood left over from a project. He picked out several pieces, grabbed a handful of screws and his cordless drill and ran back to the living room.

"Sharon, hold these while I screw them up."

She stood next to him, and together they sealed the hole. Only then did Robert stop to talk to Robbie.

"You okay, Buddy? I wasn't ignoring you, but I had to close this up."

"It's okay, Dad." Robbie tried to smile. "You rescued me! You're a…a hero. My hero!"

Robert blinked back tears. "You sure you're okay?" Robbie nodded. "Well, let's get the other two windows covered before another one of those dead bastards tries to grab someone else."

They boarded up the other windows then went to the kitchen to get something to eat. Robert lit a propane camping lantern and turned it up high to chase all the shadows from the room. Robbie set plates and silverware at the table while Robert and Sharon prepared the food, working together as though they had done so all their lives.

They were seated at the table, eating, when the radio burst back to life, causing all three to jump. A reporter, his voice edged with panic, was rattling off reports of towns and cities being attacked all over the world. Everything was in a state of disarray, but the station would stay on the air as long as their generator held out.

The three sat at the table long into the night, listening to the radio and discussing what to do. Finally, Robbie's eyelids began to sag, and he yawned loudly. "Dad, can I go lay down on the couch?"

"Yes, son, you can."

Robbie stretched out and was soon asleep. Robert looked across the table at Sharon, who was smiling fondly at Robbie's sleeping form. "Kids," he said, "they bounce back, don't they?" Sharon nodded. "Do you have any kids?"

"One, but he's, ah…he's gone."

Robert was afraid he'd hit a nerve. He knew that in his life, gone meant dead. "I'm sorry, Sharon, I don't mean to pry. It's just—"

"Don't worry, Rob." She smiled at him. "It's okay."

"Sue was the only person who ever called me Rob."

"Seriously, Rob, what are we going to do?"

"Well, Robbie and I have a small cabin on a lake about a hundred miles north of here. In the morning we will pack all the food here, and the food from Mr. Bailey's apartment and—"

"All of us? You just met me."

Robert felt his face flush. "I…well, I guess I assumed you would want to go."

"I think we should cover Robbie up, don't you? It's still a little chilly in here."

"I put the quilt back on the bed."

"I'll go get it."

Sharon stepped into the bedroom and smiled. All around her were reminders of her previous life. She ran her hand along the wooden headboard and snuggled the quilt up against her cheek, inhaling the familiar scents of the old fabrics.

It was time, she decided, to tell them not everything that happened tonight was bad.

The End

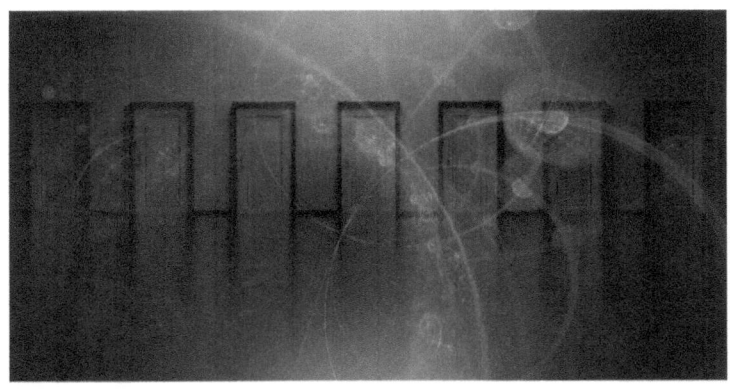

TIME BENDERS

The rat-a-tat-tat of anti-aircraft rounds sounded like a sewing machine through a megaphone. The plane came in low, and Monk knew it was going to hit. He also knew there wasn't a damn thing he could do about it. Still, he fired the big gun over and over. Maybe this time…

The plane exploded in a thousand flaming pieces, and the deck of the ship was engulfed in an orange ball from hell. Even above the roar of the guns Monk could hear the screams. He hated the screams. He hated the Kamikazes. He hated the carnage, the destruction and the loss of his shipmates' lives.

Monk also hated the winged ones, the dark creatures that rode on the back of the Kamikazes' planes. That's how he always knew which ones would hit and which would not.

When the attack was over, Monk climbed down from the turret. Firemen were hosing the deck with giant water cannons, sweeping debris from the death planes off into the foaming depths of the sea. Injured men lay awaiting triage, burns, mostly. All hands not occupied with the essential functions of the ship were helping tend the wounded.

"Hey, sailor!" a voice bellowed. Monk spun on one heel. It was Chief Petty Officer Bill Chamnus, from Chicago. Monk knew him well and had served with him through three tours now. The chief was a huge man, six foot, four, and well over three hundred pounds. "Monk! Give a man a hand, lad! Grab the other end of this stretcher and let's get this kid down to the infirmary."

The kid the chief referred to lay belly down on a stretcher a few feet away. Most of his backside was charcoal black. Fortunately, the young sailor was passed out.

"Damn those little yellow bastards," the chief growled. "This kid's bad, damn bad. You got a few, right Monk?" Monk stopped looking down at the charred kid. "You always get 'em, don't you, Monk? Best killer diller shot in the Navy, aren't you, boy?"

Monk barely heard the chief. He was staring off down the plank. One of the winged ones was on the deck, just fifty feet away! As he watched, the creature slithered away down the walk, a giant black iridescent beast, almost like a dragon, but with a human face. Monk gasped.

"You getting sick, sailor? Monk? Monk, you okay?"

The chief's thundering voice snapped Monk back to the task at hand. "Ah, ah, I'm okay," he mumbled. "I just…"

"Just pick up the end of the damn stretcher, sailor!"

"Aye, aye, sir." Monk grabbed the stretcher and hoisted. When he looked back, the creature was slipping through a hatch leading down into the ship. "Aw, shit," he muttered.

"Aw, shit, is right," the chief spat. "This whole thing is a crock of shit. They leave us out here like sitting ducks! Hell, Monk, if it weren't for you, there would be a lot more of this. Old Monk! Shoot 'em down Monk!"

Monk and the chief hauled the injured sailor down the walk and into the ship, the chief shouting orders the whole way. They handed the kid off to the medical staff and Monk turned to go, but the chief laid a giant paw on his shoulder. "Hey, kid," he said in a low tone, "you okay? This shit getting to you?" There was genuine concern in the chief's big blue eyes.

Monk searched his face. How could he tell him? "Hell, no, chief. Burritos. I had burritos for lunch, and I don't think they sat well. I'll go get some bicarbonate, and I'll be all right." With that, Monk turned and trotted off.

"Burritos, my ass," the chief grunted to himself. "We had ham."

But Monk had a bigger problem than the chief. One of those things was loose on board the ship, and as far as he knew, he was the only one who knew about it—and the only one who could see it. Behind him, he heard the chief yell, "Monk, see me later!"

It always amazed Monk how fast things returned to normal after an attack. The debris was cleaned up, shells reloaded, damage repaired and, first and foremost, the injured tended. Life went on, the world continued to turn. The ship was an efficient factory, run like a well-oiled machine, but instead of turning out cars or washers, it turned out war, war on a grand scale.

As he searched the ship, Monk wondered if he would ever see home again. Would he ever hold his newborn daughter? Nearly a year old, she was not so newly born now. Over the months he'd lost count of the planes he'd shot down and the battles he'd seen, but he vividly remembered the first time he saw one of the winged ones.

They were three days out of Pearl Harbor. The bomber came in fast that time, and Monk just happened to be on the turret when he spotted the plane. He swung from the barrel of the big gun, did a full summersault and landed solidly in a stoop. With the agility of a monkey, he bounded forward and landed in the gunner's seat. It was that move, and the many like it since, that earned him his nickname Monk. He was no longer Martin

Fieleke from Illinois, he was Monk, the gunner, and a damn good one, too.

That day opened a new chapter in his world. He'd shot down the bomber, but the Kamikazes came in behind it. The rear one had one of the winged ones perched on top. At first he wasn't sure what it was. From a distance, he thought it was some new device, radar, maybe. But when it detached itself from the plane and flew away, Monk saw it up close. The beast sailed right over the turret and smiled as the Japanese plane exploded on the deck.

Since then he had seen many of them, and each time they were perched on the fuselage, right above the pilot. The planes with the winged ones were always the planes that hit and always, seconds before impact, the beast would glide off. Flapping leathery wings, it would disappear into the distance.

Monk mentioned it once to another gunner, who looked at him like he was nuts. Monk started laughing. "Got you!" he said. Two days later the young gunner, also from Illinois, was killed. Since that incident, Monk kept what he saw to himself.

But now one was on board. That had never happened before, at least not that he knew of. He wasn't sure what to do, if anything. He had tried to shoot them, but the shells from the fifty caliber gun just bounced off. And he hadn't wanted to attract too much attention by making it look like he was specifically aiming at them. Did they know he could see them? He couldn't be sure. Hell, he didn't even know what they were. Or how many of them there were. Or where they came from. He didn't know anything about them at all, except that they could fly.

So he searched the ship, up and down, fore to aft. He couldn't find the creature anywhere. He was about to give up and return to his rack when a still, small voice sounded from behind a lifeboat.

"Didn't find it, did you?" Monk's head snapped around. The voice was soft and mild, almost subdued. Monk turned as the chief rose from the upturned bucket he had been using as a stool. "I know where it is." Monk's blood ran cold. Clutched in the chief's fist was a forty-five caliber pistol aimed squarely at Monk's chest. Monk didn't move. He didn't dare.

***

Monk faced a simple but deadly dilemma. Rush the chief and try to disarm him, or stand and be shot. The hammer was back on the forty-five. Monk felt himself being weighed.

Though a brave man and strong, Monk knew that even without the gun, Chief Chamnus could kill him with ease. A huge man who moved like a cat, rumor had it the chief was some sort of Judo champ. Once, before they were sent to the Pacific, they were loading prisoners from a disabled German U-boat. The chief was at the end of the gangplank watching the prisoners pass by when one of them pulled a Luger. Before the German could level the weapon, the chief twisted it from his hand.

Monk was close enough to hear the bones pop. The German tried to hit him, but the chief chopped him across the throat, knocking him off into the water. When they fished him out, the man was dead, his windpipe crushed. The whole episode had taken less than a heartbeat. Monk knew exactly how deadly the man in front of him was.

A slow smile spread across the chief's face, and Monk felt the weight lift from his chest. "Naw, I guess *you* wouldn't know. Pull up a bucket, lad. Have a seat." The chief lowered the forty-five and gently eased the hammer down. Monk breathed a sigh of relief. The chief pointed to a mop bucket. "Go ahead. Sit lad, sit down."

The chief pulled two cigars from his breast pocket. "Smoke," he ordered. "Got a box of these bastards in Havana last year. Smooth as whale shit on greased glass." The chief held out one of those new-fangled Zippo lighters. "Light?" Monk lit the stogie and pulled the smoke in deep. He looked calmly at the chief. The big officer grinned. "Glad I didn't have to shoot you."

Monk chuckled. "Me too."

"So, kid, you know?"

"Yeah, chief, I know."

Both men pulled long and hard on their cigars.

"So, Chief, what do we do?"

"That, I don't know. I don't know at all, but rest assured of one thing. We will find that leathery flying son of a bitch and send it right back to the hell from which it came!"

25

"But chief, we're not—"

An explosion rocked the big ship sideways. Monk flipped backward off his makeshift stool but was up in a flash. The chief didn't lose his balance but had to struggle to rise.

"What the hell—"

The lifeboat boom must have broken free in the explosion. Monk never saw it coming. It caught him square in the back of the head and sent him sailing through the air. The sea rose in slow motion to meet him. Monk waited for the shattering impact, but it never came. Instead, he felt as though he'd fallen into a thousand pillows. A deep, all-consuming darkness covered him. He was floating and then…nothing.

***

Monk awoke to the stink of seawater in his nose and to a sailor that only means one thing—Monk had been in the drink. He squinted against the daylight and groaned as he raised his hand to his head.

"Whoa, lad, steady as she goes." Monk tried to sit up, but the chief held him down on the cool sand. "Stay flat, boy. You've got a nasty bump on your ol' head. Thought you were gone there, for a bit, after I pulled you out of old Davy Jones' locker."

"Locker, ahh, water…I, ah…"

The chief snickered. "You went over the side, you dumb ass. The boat got hit."

Monk rolled to one side. Resting his head on his arm, he could see a lifeboat a few yards away, tied off to a piece of driftwood. He and the chief were alone on a long stretch of beach.

"Boy, you gave me a scare. You okay?"

"Well, I guess. My head's not hurting much." Monk raised his hand to the knot, pressing it gingerly through the dressing. He winced. "You work fast, chief."

"Fast? Hah! We need water, Monk. If you're okay, I'm gonna scout around."

"Chief, there's three or four days supply on the lifeboat."

"Was, boy. We've been adrift for five."

"Five days!" Monk tried again to sit up. "There is no way in hell I—"

"Five days, almost six," the chief said, "and *stay down*. You start that head oozing again, and I'm going to thump it myself!"

"Five days. What happened, chief? The ship?"

"Well, boy," the chief began, then he was on his feet in a flash, the forty-five gripped tight in his fist. He stepped around Monk as though trying to shield him.

Monk could barely see around the big sailor and tried to crawl to the side for a better position. Vertigo took hold, and he nearly vomited, but finally he was able to see what concerned the chief.

Thirty feet away stood a strange man. Old, he was, maybe the oldest man Monk had ever seen. His platinum beard hung well below his waist, and his skin was bleached purest white. His eyes were crystal blue and sharp as nails, but there were lines around them that suggested laughter. The man wore a long thick robe that appeared to be one piece woven from top to bottom, and his gliding movements were not those of a broken down old man.

And next to the old man, looking for all the world as though it were taking a Sunday stroll down Michigan Avenue, was one of the winged ones.

Monk was speechless. The white-haired elder was not. "Gentlemen, I hope your arrival was none too traumatic. Monk your head injury is better?"

"Uh—Uh—"

"Your head injury is not better?"

The chief growled. "We'd better have some answers quick, or he won't be the only one with a head injury."

The man and the creature showed no concern. "Chief Chamnus, you will shoot neither me nor my friend. It is not going to happen."

"Oh, yeah?" the chief spat. "Want to bet a damn dollar?"

The beast growled deep and guttural, not loud. For the first time since Monk had known the chief, he saw concern on the big man's face—he wasn't exactly afraid, but he was definitely uneasy.

"Here, now," the elder admonished. "There is no need for such language. My friend shall not tolerate such things. He will not have it. Do you understand Mr. Chamnus?"

"Ah," the chief stammered, clearly taken aback, "ah, I, yeah. God— Yes, okay, I'll watch the tongue. I mean…"

"Good, good," the elder said. "Now, let's get down to brass tacks, as you young folks say today. We brought you here for a purpose. You two are the only ones who can stop the rebels. One of you will not come back from the loop. One will, but that should not concern you now."

"Whoa, whoa." The chief held up his hand and shook his head. "We two ain't going anywhere to stop nobody—"

"Anyone. The proper usage is 'anyone' and *ain't* is entirely unacceptable. It is not even a word, or at least not a proper word."

Monk's eyes widened. The English lesson came from the beast. Not only did he speak English, he spoke high English, like the frigging King of England!

"Sh—" The chief strangled the curse short. "It speaks!"

"It?" The beast drew its head back and looked down its nose at the chief. "While I may not be made in the image of the Creator, I am hardly an *it*, sir. I am Lord Wilson, a Time Bender, and I was born before—"

"Now, Wilson," the elder said, "your pedigree is not in question. The chief's only experience with your kind thus far has been with the rebels and, after all, he *is* the reason there are two less. Not an easy feat." The elder turned to look at Monk and the chief. "The rebels are what Monk refers to as the winged ones."

Monk looked at the chief with new respect. "You killed two of them? I'll be da—" He bit his tongue, remembering the leathery guy's disdain for foul language.

"No, you will not be damned—if you can stop the rebels. Otherwise, you will be damned, you and all your kind from now until this dispensation ends."

"Look," said the chief, "we are just a couple of poor sailors. Please tell us what is going on."

"I'll show you." Before the chief could move, the beast wrapped a huge leathery wing around the big man's waist and drew him near. The beast then placed his palm against the chief's forehead, and the big man went slack. Monk tried to move, but couldn't. A bright light burst forth from the beast's hand, enveloping the chief. It was over in an instant, and the chief jerked upright.

"Oh, well, now I see. Absolutely," the chief said. "It is all quite clear. I fully comprehend the parameters of the task we must undertake and I am unshakable in my resolve to see that task fulfilled."

"What the fu—"

The chief held up his hand. "Language, Monk, is a gift from God and should not be squandered on useless babble and profanity. By the way, it is a great pleasure to see you. Come, we have an appointment." The chief reached down to help Monk rise.

"But…but my head!"

"Your head is fine."

Monk felt his head. The lump was gone. He grasped the chief's hand and was yanked to his feet. The vertigo was gone. As a matter of fact, Monk felt better than he had in a long time and he followed as the chief walked away down the beach.

"Chief," Monk finally said, stopping only after they were out of sight of the old timer and the beast, "Chief what the hell—" the chief shot Monk a sharp glance. Monk rolled his eyes. "I mean, what the heck is going on? One minute you're the old chief, and now you're talking like a college professor. And that winged thing, Lord Willy, or whatever the hell—I mean heck!" Monk threw up his hands in consternation. "Damn it, chief, I need some answers, like, for starters, what did they do to you?"

"Nothing," the chief replied, and continued walking down the beach. "Nothing at all."

Monk hurried to catch up with him. "Bet me, chief! We—" Monk stopped short with an expression of disbelief on his face. Ten feet away from them was a door. There was no house, no hut, no wall, just a door, and the chief was reaching for the handle.

"Chief!" Monk pleaded. He grabbed the big man by the arm and would have spun him around if he'd had the strength. The chief laid his huge hand over Monk's hand.

"Son, you are going to have to trust me."

At the calm resolve in the chief's voice, Monk knew there was nothing he could do but follow. The chief turned the knob and opened the door. He stepped through, and Monk followed, but before his foot cleared the threshold Monk wished he'd never seen that door.

***

Monk had lived much of his life on the edge. The last couple of years he'd been way out there, but what he saw now was far beyond anything he'd ever encountered in the pulp horror magazines he liked to read and the terror welling up in his chest was far beyond any fear he'd ever felt in the gun turret. The human mind can only stand so much. When it goes into overload, it shuts down and often times it takes its owner with it. So it was with Monk.

As he and the chief cleared the door facing, they left the solid reality of the beach behind. Through the door, the world turned dark, then light. They were still walking—well, the chief was walking, he had to drag Monk along behind him.

Sound echoed around them as though it were bouncing from the walls of an enormous tunnel. Images appeared. To Monk's right sat a vehicle unlike any he had ever seen. Slung low to the ground, the windows were slits he could barely see into. Over the car, a pterodactyl swooped low. The driver appeared utterly oblivious to the obvious threat. To Monk's left stood a medieval knight, armor gleaming in the sunlight, even though Monk could not see any sun. The metal-clad warrior paid no mind to Monk and the chief as he squared off against an unseen opponent.

They moved further in. Off to the right Monk saw a Samurai practicing his sword strokes while school children played ball and jumped rope all around him. Another pterodactyl flew overhead, passing through low boiling clouds. Occasional crunching sounds prompted Monk to look down. All around their feet swirled six-inch roaches. Monk grimaced, but the chief's grip on his arm forced him to keep moving.

At the horizon the light bent into dark and light hues, deep reds and dark blues, always turning, churning, changing. Monk felt sick.

They came upon Roman legions marching to war past a stage where four young girls sang "When You Wish Upon a Star." The melody stretched and compressed as though passing through waves of water.

Monk flinched when a Japanese Zero flew over their heads, and he heard the whistle of bombs falling, but there were never any explosions. Hitler's legions marched their stiff-legged beats past an oddly shaped plane mounted on a giant rocket, and lions grazed in the center of Stonehenge. The images began coming at them faster and faster. Monk's mind began to bend, but it was what he saw next that finally caused it to snap.

Out of the churning darkness rose a form, not well defined. It looked much like the winged ones but was considerably larger. It's edges blended with the eternally black pool in which it swam, its form passing from solid to plasma and back. Its eyes, red glowing orbs of coal with a small black dot in the middle of each, bore down into Monks being, twisting their pure unadulterated evil into his deepest fibers, caressing his very soul with their filth.

Then came the laughter. Maniacal, maddening laughter. Planes roared overhead, bombs whistled somewhere in the distance, men marched and music played, but above all the chaos Monk could hear the insane laughter. At first, he thought it was coming from the beast, but with his last sliver of sanity, he realized it was coming from himself.

The chief turned and slammed a massive fist into Monk's jaw. A bright hot light exploded, and Monk slipped off into blessed darkness.

***

When Monk awoke, his head was pounding. Once again he lay on the beach, the chief standing over him.

"Sweet mother! Ah, hell, chief, I had the damndest dream!"

"Monk, in a moment a Coast Guard cutter will pass by. We will wave them down. We will have to lie." Monk rolled his eyes wildly, and the chief sighed. "*I* will have to lie, you should remain silent. I will tell them you have a head injury. Monk?" The chief sounded stern. "Monk, do you understand? Look at me, son."

The chief spoke in the same professorial tone he'd used before. That meant the tunnel was real. The beach was real. It was all real. Those eyes! Those evil, vicious eyes! Sparks swam at the edges of his vision and Monk couldn't breathe through the sharp pains in his chest.

Something of his distress must have shown on his face because the chief quickly knelt beside him, pulled up his shirt and shoved his ear to Monk's chest. Expertly, though inexplicably, the chief rolled Monk over on his right side. He ran his hand down Monk's spine and, finding the proper place, he shoved a big thumb into Monk's vertebra. Suddenly Monk could breathe and in a moment his chest pain subsided. Satisfied with his breathing, the chief rolled Monk back over and placed his huge hand over Monk's face, his thumb on one temple and his middle finger on the other. He applied moderate pressure and Monk's panic dissipated.

"Hell's bells, chief, that was damn—"

The chief winced. "Monk, please watch the language."

"Yea, yea," Monk said. "Chief, what is going on?"

"Monk, you have to trust me."

Monk started to say something else, but just then the Coast Guard ship came into sight, and the chief began waving his hands frantically. The ship was a small rescue vessel, capable of traversing shallow water, but it still had to send out a dingy to pick up Monk and the chief. Even at a distance, the ship looked strange to Monk, and it had some interesting gadgets Monk had never seen.

Two crew members were on board. One was obviously an enlisted man, and the other turned out to be the captain.

"Doctor Adam, am I glad we found you!" The captain stepped out of the dingy and waded the last few feet to greet them. "I'm Captain Howards, Coast Guard rescue. We thought you went to the bottom with your vessel, sir. It's a damn good thing you turned on that G.P.S. beacon. I'm sure you know these waters are full of sharks. You two are just doggone lucky!"

"Well, Captain," the chief said in his newly cultured voice, "my assistant and I are well. Our research vessel cracked up and went down out in deep water, but we are okay, although my assistant has sustained a pretty nasty bump." The chief turned Monk's head so the Captain could see the huge knot the chief's fist made when he cold-conked him in the tunnel. "He is somewhat out of sorts, not quite himself, I believe. He will be fine, but we need to get back to the mainland and find him a place to rest."

"Doc, we've got a great hospital on the island! We can—"

"No, no. My assistant, Monk, and I have been together for a long time, and I insist on caring for him myself. I am not trying to be ungrateful, Captain, but along with my Ph.D. in Oceanography, I am also a medical doctor."

"Okay, Doc," the captain said. "You're the boss. Whatever you say, that was part of my orders," he paused for a moment and looked at the chief curiously, "and those orders, Doctor, came down from the top."

They climbed into the dingy and started toward the ship. Monk looked curiously at the flat face of the radio when the enlisted man spoke into the mike. "It's a positive. We have 'em both, over." Monk opened his mouth to ask about the newfangled device, but a glance from the chief made him think again.

Something on the Captain's belt made a buzzing noise. The Captain removed it, flipped it open and began to speak. After a moment the blood drained from his face. "Yes, sir, Mr. President… ah, yes, sir… I will, sir… Fine sir, absolutely, sir… No problem, Mr. President. Good-bye, Mr. President." The Captain was pale when he turned to look at the chief. "Ah, Dr. Adams, that was the president, and when you get back to the mainland, he requested you contact him in the usual way."

"Thank you, Captain. And, Captain?" The captain looked at the chief with a mixture of dread and awe on his face. "I will make sure he knows how well you treated us and I am sure he'll be appreciative."

"Ah, thank you, sir. Please, just let me know if you need anything, anything at all!"

The boat pulled alongside the larger vessel. The captain was already shouting orders as they were pulled aboard. A few minutes later Monk and the chief sat alone in a spacious cabin. It seemed luxurious to Monk, and he was sure it was the captain's. A television was playing.

Monk had seen one before, but not so clear and not in *color*.

"Chief, look at this! I didn't know anything like this existed. This is some kind of top-secret deal, right?"

"No," the chief said, but Monk barely heard him. The news report flashed a war scene from someplace. Iraq. Monk had heard of it, but that was not what concerned him. At the bottom of the screen was what appeared to be a date. August 15, 2005.

"Uh, Chief, this is funny. This thing says August 2005."

"It's no joke," the chief said. "This is August 2005."

"Ah, sh…" Monk swallowed it, but he could feel his chest tighten.

"Take it easy, Monk." The chief placed his hand on the back of Monk's neck and pinched. Once again Monk's vision went black, and he slipped into blessed darkness.

***

Monk awoke in a house. At least from what he could see, Monk thought it was a house. He was lying on a bed. His chest was no longer tight. He was relaxed and felt well, so he sat up.

There were two doors in the room. They looked normal, but he remembered what had happened the last time he went through a door. He stood in the center of the room for a moment then chose one. He hesitated as he reached for the knob. He didn't want any more surprises, but he felt alone without the chief. In one quick movement, he twisted the knob and flung the door open. Clothes. There were a few empty hangers mixed in with the clothes and a neat row of shoes on the floor. He rolled his eyes and shut the door.

When he opened the other one, there was a normal room and a normal couch on the other side. On the normal couch sat the chief, who wasn't so normal anymore. He wasn't moving. He seemed to be asleep, but his eyes were open. For a brief, terrible moment Monk thought the chief might be dead. The horror of that thought almost drove Monk over the edge. What would he do? How would he get home? Monk was sure the chief knew these answers. Something had happened to him on the beach. The chief was different, more...

"Complete."

"Yeah," Monk muttered, "complete. Hey! How did you do that? Chief, you know, I'm just..."

"Confused," the chief finished softly.

"Yeah, yeah, you did it again."

The chief waved a hand toward a big overstuffed chair. Monk flopped down in it, then felt guilty for abusing the furniture. The chief smiled. "Monk, it's all about time."

"Time for what?" Monk was becoming irritated, though he didn't know why.

"No, no, Monk. Calm down. Everything is about time." At Monk's puzzled look, the chief continued.

"Look, the reason time exists is because, if it did not, everything would be happening at once. There would be pandemonium. Dinosaurs would be flying down Lake Shore Drive in Chicago and gladiators would be fighting in Saint Peter's Basilica. Hitler would be marching through the Celts and the Gauls. There is an order to things on this plane. Without that order, which is time, there would be chaos."

"Like in the tunnel," Monk mumbled.

"Yes, like in the tunnel. This plane of existence would be just like the tunnel, chaos and entropy would rule without the constraints of time. It would be Hell," the chief added, "real Hell."

"I see. But what does any of this have to do with us, with me?"

"On the beach, we met two beings."

"You mean the old man and the monster?" Monk spat.

"Well, Monk, that is not really an accurate assessment. The old man, as you call him, is a Watcher."

"A what?"

"A Watcher is, was, a man who has taken on a new essence, a new purpose. He is still a man, but different. He observes, categorizes and keeps track of events, of time. The monster, as you referred to him, is a Time Bender." Monk shook his head, and the chief elaborated. "A Time Bender is actually more of a time manipulator, a stopper and starter of time. He and his kind ensure that time runs properly, continuously, uninterrupted and unmolested."

"Okay, Chief, but I know something is up, or we wouldn't be here, wherever here is."

"You are right, Monk, something is up. The Time Benders are an ancient order ordained by the Great and True God, to serve His purpose, to avoid chaos. But some have rebelled, chosen a different path, a path of destruction, damnation. They would, if possible, destroy all of God's creation. You cannot allow that to happen."

Monk's eyes widened. "Me?! What about you?"

The chief sighed. "Alas, Monk, I can no longer interfere."

"Interfere! Interfere?! Chief, this is your fight too!"

"No longer." The chief's voice dropped to nearly a whisper. "I am a Watcher."

"A Watcher?" Monk threw up his hands. "When did this happen?"

"Long ago, Monk. Years, decades ago."

Monk rolled his eyes. "Uh, Chief, five days ago, well, five days before we went through the Hell tunnel, you were Bill Chamnus, Chief Petty Officer, U.S. Navy. Remember?"

The chief smiled. "Yes Monk, I remember quite well. But that was before...my education, my transformation. Monk, it was two hundred years ago, at least in my mind."

"Chief, you're starting to scare me. I mean, I went through the same door you did, and it seems like yesterday. I..." Monk stopped, unable to come up with a better argument than the obvious.

"It seems like yesterday to me, also, Monk. As a matter of fact, it was yesterday. We left 1945 and skipped right to 2005, a sixty-year jump. That is not what I'm talking about. When Lord Wilson touched me on the beach, it may have seemed like a moment to you, but I was gone for over two hundred years. I went to school, if you will. I was educated by many of the great masters of learning, mystics of a sort. I—"

"How were you there? I could see you."

"The Time Benders can alter time. You see, Monk, time on this plane is linear. I traveled along on a path from 1905, my birth year, to 1945, the year we landed on the beach. A straight line." Monk nodded. "Lord Wilson removed me from that time, set me on another plane, on another path in a place where I did not age. While there I did not have many of the restraints we have here in this realm. When my time there was over, Lord Wilson simply took me back to the beach and reinserted me. While it appeared to you that I was not gone at all, in truth I was gone over two hundred years."

"Two hundred years?"

"Two hundred glorious years. I long to return and will, when you stop the renegade."

"Whoa, Chief—do folks still call you Chief?"

The chief smiled. "You may call me Chief, Monk."

"So, why me?"

"You were chosen. And I cannot directly participate in any act against a time bender, not even a renegade."

Monk and the chief sat in silence while Monk tried to process all that the chief had told him. Finally, he squared his shoulders and said, "okay, Chief. Let's get going. We'll do whatever it takes. I just have one question. Is it really 2005, the year, I mean?"

"Yes, Monk."

"Well, let's hope we don't run into ourselves." The chief smiled uneasily. "Chief, we are here, right? I mean, just a lot older?"

"Monk, matter cannot occupy two different spaces at the same time. Neither of us is here."

Monk looked uneasy. "You mean in 2005 I'm dead?" he asked softly. "So are you, right? Tell me if I'm wrong."

The chief smiled a little. "Not exactly, Monk. You will see."

"Ah, hell—I mean heck—no one lives forever."

The chief laughed, a hearty laugh, one Monk hadn't heard in a while. "Now, boy, you are wrong," he bellowed, sounding much like the old petty officer Monk knew, "wrong as can be! We all live forever, the question is *where!*"

***

The air was cold, but Monk was sweating. They had to be at least six thousand feet up, and the trail ahead looked as though it would wind into the clouds. The wind howled, foreshadowing the arrival of an early autumn storm. At this latitude and elevation snow could be expected any time of the year.

Monk had seen much in the two days it had taken them to travel from the west coast to the lofty mountain heights of the Montana wilds, and he knew one thing for sure. If he ever got back to his time, that is, if he lived, no one would ever believe him. The new technologies and communications, the state of social affairs in America... The only comfort he had was that America had won the war.

He wondered what his children were doing. How many did he have? Boys? Another girl? Grandkids? Before this, Monk had never given much thought to the future. Now he was living it. Perhaps dying it.

Monk pulled his thermos from his pack and set the pack on the ground beside him. He screwed the top off and poured a cup of hot coffee. Blonde with two sugars, that's how Monk liked his joe. When he ordered it at an all-night diner in Idaho, the waitress had no idea what he was talking about. He just wanted cream and sugar with his coffee. The chief had to explain it to the waitress. Things had really changed.

"Chief, are you sure about all this?"

"Most sure, Monk."

Monk felt at his side for the chief's forty-five and chuckled. "Hey, Chief, this ammo is over sixty years old. Think it will fire?"

"It's not the same ammunition, Monk. Mine became wet."

"I was trying to make a joke."

"Oh."

The chief smiled, but Monk could tell he was preoccupied.

"So let me get this straight. When we get to this cave, a door will be there. When the door opens, and the rebel Time Bender comes through, I shoot him in the *head*. He disintegrates. We go back through the door to good old 1945 and then we are home free."

"That is fairly accurate, Monk."

"Sounds easy. I just have one question. This Doctor Adam, the guy you are impersonating, where is he?"

"Nowhere. He is a made up person, a front, if you will, an identity created by the Watchers to allow us to operate in this era."

"Operate?"

"Yes, Monk. We must be able to move about undetected, to observe and catalog. And there are times, in cases such as this, when we must be able to arrange for an intervention."

"Intervention? Don't you mean a bushwhacking?"

The chief chuckled. "I guess that's one way to put it."

"I tell you, I can't wait to put some lead in that leathery bast—thing."

"Monk," the chief said, turning to look at him, "you must not think of these beings in that manner. The Time Benders are a beautiful and ancient race. They have dutifully and effectively carried out the will of God for eons. It is a sorrowful occasion when one must die, even if it is a rebellious one."

Monk was a little taken back at the chief's passion. This was the strongest emotion he had shown since he'd turned. "I...I'm sorry, Chief. I just don't see it..."

"That is because you can't see them in their true form. If you did, you would feel differently."

The chief turned and started up the path again. It was 10:30 in the morning and they both knew they had no time to dawdle. Monk glanced up at the sky. The clouds were building up to one hell of a storm.

***

Annie sat just inside the mouth of the cave. She had dialed 911 on her phone until the battery went dead but had only managed a fifteen-second conversation with the dispatcher. Hopefully, it was enough. She wished she had stayed home. This was stupid. She knew it was, but she'd had to prove to herself she could do it. Now, she had lost all of her food and water and she'd most likely broken her ankle. The griz was still out there and, to make matters worse, it was wounded.

"It's a thirty caliber pistol," she whispered to herself. "A freaking rifle cartridge in a handgun. It's a hand cannon!"

But the big griz was not dead, and Annie knew it would come for her. She checked the big pistol. It had been her dad's. He gave it to her right before he died. It was hard to believe he'd been gone for so long. If he were here, he'd know what to do. She chuckled at herself through the pain. If he were here, this wouldn't have happened. First off, he wouldn't have let her go on this crazy hike alone, and *he* would have killed the bear. She wondered if he'd ever hunted bear. There were no bears in Illinois, but her dad had traveled a lot—before his heart went bad, that is.

For a moment, thinking about her dad, Annie forgot about the pain and the danger. Then she heard a rock fall. Something was moving, close. Fear gripped her chest. As a nurse, she had seen pain and suffering. She knew what happened to a bear attack victim. She hoped it would be quick, though she knew that was rarely the case. There were three shots left in the big pistol. One would do for her. "No!" she muttered fiercely. "By gosh, if I'm going down, I'm going down swinging! That's the way Dad would have gone."

Annie rose from behind the boulder where she'd been hiding, spinning toward the sound as she did. She shoved the big pistol in front of her and cocked the hammer just as two men stepped into view.

"Oh, my," said the bigger one, "this I did not foresee."

Annie noticed several things at once. Above her, the skies had turned black as pitch. Lightning flashed, but there was no thunder. Also, both men looked out of place, though she wasn't sure just why. Behind her a light popped like a flashbulb on a camera, she caught it from the corner of her eye. The smaller man looked familiar, but Annie knew a lot of people. The most immediate issue, to her eye anyway, was that about a hundred yards behind the two men, the bear was charging fast.

***

The woman screamed and pointed behind them. Monk swiveled on one foot. "Ah, shit!" Monk winced as the cuss word slipped out, but didn't have time to worry about it. "Chief, that's a bear! It's hurt! It's pissed off, too!"

The chief charged forward, shoving past the woman to the mouth of the cave. As he looked in there came a second flash from the back of the cave. Monk stepped around the woman just as the second flash occurred. In the blink of an eye a door appeared. As the door opened, the crimson light of the hell tunnel spilled out into the cave. Then the rebel Time Bender stepped through and flexed its leathery wings. Beneath its wings protruded two powerful arms ending in huge hands and at the end of its fingers hung ten claws of which any grizzly would have been proud. The rebel smiled, as though pleased with the company, and headed straight for them.

"Ah, Chief," Monk said, as he tried to watch both advancing enemies at once, "did you foresee this?"

With admirable calm, the chief simply replied, "No, Monk. No, I did not."

The woman looked at him, startled. "Monk?" she whispered. "Monk was my dad's name." She swayed on her feet and almost dropped the gun. Monk grabbed it from her hands. It was a thirty caliber, and it was cocked. As the woman fell, the chief caught her and eased her to the ground.

The rebel saw the bear the same time the bear saw the rebel. Monk decided the bear had never seen a Time Bender before, because, even hurt and crazy, the bear stopped for a brief second. At that moment Monk decided it was now or never. With one quick fluid motion, he lived up to his nickname. He drew the chief's forty-five auto and held it with his left hand, then jumped up, planting both feet squarely on the boulder and forcing his lean frame into a backflip. He had to make it work. If the rebel got loose in the year 2005, he would use something called a computer to manipulate time to a standstill and the world would end in chaos. The chief had explained it all.

Monk's legs rose over his head, and his body turned in mid-air. He crossed his arms, a gun in each fist. He was as high now as he'd ever be, and the angle was just right as he straightened out from the backflip. The thirty caliber spoke first, and Monk knew instinctively that the bullet had hit home. The forty-five bucked next, twice, and both rounds caught the leathery creature in the head. Monk hit the ground. Lightning exploded from the Time Benders skull as the big griz fell dead at Monk's feet.

The chief started to help the woman rise just as the rebel exploded into a million points of light. The woman's eyes went wide, and she passed out again. The chief laid her back down, then stood looking down at the bear. "A beautiful animal. It is unfortunate."

"Fortunate for us, though."

The chief chuckled. "I suppose you are correct. Well done, Monk."

A new flash of light appeared in the shallow cave. Monk thumb cocked the thirty caliber pistol and raised both guns, pointing them toward the light. "Here we go again!" he hissed.

The chief's arm came down gently across Monk's forearms. "No need for that, son," he said softly. Lord Wilson and the white-bearded elder stepped out of the light.

"It is done," said the chief.

"So be it," Lord Wilson replied.

"It is a sad thing," the elder sighed, "a sad thing indeed." He looked at Monk and smiled. "Monk, you are a brave man, as brave as there are in all the worlds."

Monk didn't feel brave. He had done what he'd always done—what he *had* to. He looked down at the woman. She was pretty. She looked about fifty, maybe a little younger. She had a pleasant look about her, and a familiarity that haunted Monk. Somehow he felt as though he knew her.

Lord Wilson took a step forward. The white-haired elder put a hand out to stop him.

"No George," the Time Bender said firmly, "he has earned it, and more." The Time Bender held his hand out to Monk. "Take it, please."

Lord Wilson's voice echoed in his head as Monk clasped his leathery fingers and the world exploded.

Monk lived a lifetime in a second. He saw Lord Wilson in his true form surrounded by a rainbow of light, a more beautiful and noble being than he could have ever imagined. He saw his wife, his family. A lifetime of work and play passed through him and at the end he saw his body in a bed surrounded by people he loved. He knew then that the woman on the ground at his feet was his daughter. In that second he knew all there was to know about their relationship and the love shared between a father and a daughter. Lord Wilson released his hand, and he collapsed next to Annie.

Monk rolled onto his side and stroked her hair, weeping. Though she appeared to be at least twenty years his senior, she was his daughter, and he loved her.

Annie woke for a brief moment. "Daddy? Oh, Daddy, I miss you so!" She tried to rise but collapsed. The shock and the pain in her ankle were too much, and she fainted again.

Monk stood. He could hear someone coming up the trail.

"We must go now," the elder, George, said.

"Now, Monk," the chief agreed.

Monk looked desperately at Lord Wilson. "You are a Time Bender! Please! One minute?"

"It doesn't work that way, Monk," Lord Wilson replied. "Those men will be here in nine minutes."

Monk looked down at his girl. "I love you, baby."

They walked into the mouth of the cave. The sky above was clearing as a new ball of lightning opened into a new tunnel. "Wait!" Monk said, realizing he still held Annie's pistol in his hand. He ran back to where she lay.

"Come, Monk!" the chief said, as loud as he dared.

Monk made them wait three minutes. When he returned, the four stepped through into the light tunnel, and everything went black for Monk.

***

Once again, Monk awoke on the beach. A navy rescue vessel was floating in the bay and Monk recognized the two sailors running toward him.

"Damn, Monk!" one of them gasped as he tried to catch his breath, "how are you?"

The other clapped him on the shoulder. "How'd you get here? Boy, we thought for sure you were gone!"

Monk looked at them, puzzled. "I, ah…what happened?"

"The boat got hit! You don't know? Monk, the ship was hit bad, but the captain says we'll be up soon. But, Monk, the Jap's surrendered! Boy, we are going home!"

"Where's the chief?"

They two sailors exchanged glances. "Chief Chamnus?" Monk nodded. "Monk, he's gone. Over the edge."

"No! He's…" Monk didn't finish. Perhaps it had all been a dream and if not, well, who would believe him?

The two sailors led Monk to the dingy. It was time to go home. Monk settled back in the dingy and dug his hands in his pockets. There was a piece of paper. Monk ripped it out. "See you in about thirty years," it said. It was signed Chief Chamnus, Lord Wilson, and George Washington.

"I'll be damned!" Monk whispered.

"No you will not," said a voice inside his head. "No, you will not!"

***

The rescuers found Annie and called for an airlift. While they were waiting, Annie drifted in and out of consciousness, calling over and over for her father each time she woke.

After two days in the hospital, Annie returned home with a cast on her ankle and a set of crutches. Aside from the fact that she'd busted her leg and embarrassed herself thoroughly, she had lost her father's gun, one of her most prized possessions. She had just settled back on the couch with coffee and a sandwich when the doorbell rang. *It's rough, living alone*, she thought as she dragged herself back upright and hobbled to the door. She peered through the peephole. The visitor was a man and in his hand was a box. Annie opened the door.

"Hello," the man said. He was tall, at least six foot, three inches, and broad through the shoulders with flecks of gray peppering his light brown hair. He seemed embarrassed. "I, uh, I was one of the rescuers on the mountain. When you killed the bear?"

"Oh! Well, come on in."

"No, ma'am, that's okay." He held out the box. "No... I just, well, I brought this back. It's your gun."

"Oh my goodness!" she gasped. "Dad's gun!"

"I knew it." The man chuckled. "I knew it belonged to your dad. At the scene, you kept calling him, over and over. I figured that's who carved on the handle.

Annie looked at him curiously. "Carved?" Annie had cleaned that gun hundreds of times and knew for a fact there was nothing carved on the handle.

"Look." The stranger opened the box and pointed at the handle. *I love you, kid*, had been scratched into the butt. Annie's eyes welled up with tears. "Are you okay?" the man asked.

"I'm fine, I just..." Annie swallowed hard and wiped the tears from her face. "Thank you. I'm sorry, but I didn't get your name."

"Oh, I'm Matthew."

"Matthew." Annie smiled at him warmly. "Would you like a cup of coffee?"

Matthew looked down at her and felt his heart warm from the sweet openness of her smile. "I would," he said.

"How do you like it?"

"Blond, with two sugars."

Annie smiled again as another tear trickled down her cheek. "I know someone else who liked it like that."

Matthew chuckled and wiped the tear from her face. "He must have been a great guy."

"He was," she said. "He was my dad."

The End

AN OLD TRADITION

He ran blindly through the dark woods. It was out there, somewhere. Finally, winded, he crouched against a tree and tried to quiet his panicked breathing. He heard a noise and jerked.

Oh crap, it's close!

Moments ago he had been driving home, comfortable and confident in his new sedan. A cool summer breeze blew through the window and music from the car radio permeated his soul. Then he saw a black streak and something hit the top of the car. He slammed on the brakes and spun into the ditch. Before he could lament the damage to his beloved car, a huge gray-green hand peeled back the roof. As it grappled for him, long claws ripped up the seat and dash like tissue paper. The claws gripped the sleeve of his jacket, and he barely got out before it tore his arm to bits.

As he slipped from the car, a massive forearm brushed against his face. The thing's skin was cold and scaly. He glanced back. Its face, dimly lit by the dashboard lights, was twisted in a sneer. He would never forget the glowing red eyes lighting up that evil face. Gargoyle came to mind. Or demon. Or monster.

"I was just driving home," he whimpered, almost silently, and then he tensed as he heard another noise.

Our Father, who art in heaven...

It had been a long time since he last prayed.

He wished for a flashlight. He thought there was one in the car, but even if he'd had time to grab it, it would probably just help the thing find him.

Why me? Lord, what is it and why is it after me? I wish I had a gun.

At home, he had a shotgun and a rifle. He even had his dad's old .45 from the war. He hadn't shot it in years, but he *could*.

A knife! I have a knife!

He pulled the pocket folder from his trousers, opened it and felt the blade.

Oh man, it's so dull!

He berated himself for not sharpening it—for not *learning* to sharpen it. Ron, at work, had a big sharp knife. He always showed the new clients how it was sharp enough to shave with.

Lord, I wish I had Ron's big knife. I wish Ron were here, he's tough! I bet he wouldn't run.

Another noise. He ran, branches slapping at his face and forearms.

There was no moon, or at least he couldn't see any moonlight. He wondered what phase the moon was in. Full, half, quarter? He didn't know, though he was sure his dad would have known.

Hell, no one pays attention to that stuff anymore.

He burst from the thick woods into an open field, breathing heavily, and fought the urge to run out across the field, looking up, instead, into the inky blackness above him. Lord, how he wished it was daylight.

At the sound of flapping wings, he dropped and rolled up against the tall grass at the edge of the field. It was a hay field, freshly mowed, and square bales still lay scattered about. He lay deathly still, listening, wondering if he should go back into the forest. He could feel his heart pumping hard, and the beat was loud in his ears.

Can it hear my heart?

The smell of fresh-cut hay reminded him of when, as a young man, he used to work summers helping a local farmer. He was strong back then, in good shape, but that was two decades ago.

A movement caught from the corner of his eye made him look up again. Against the night clouds he could just make out the darker blackness of the monster. It was humanoid, a little. The wings fixed to its back flapped like those of a giant bat. A long tail hung between its muscular legs, and its feet looked more frog than human.

Damn, I am going to die. *My wife, my kids, I won't see them again.*

The creature flew past him, toward the end of the field. He buried his face in the grass. He wished he was a rabbit—at least then he could hide in a hole.

The clouds cleared away and a quarter moon emerged, the kind you think of when you see the old Bugs Bunny cartoons. He could no longer hear wings. Was it on the ground? Did it know where he was? Could it smell him, see him? He edged forward a bit but could see nothing. He had never before been afraid of the dark, but that had changed in the last hour.

The urgent need to do *something* overwhelmed him, so he bellied out into the field. He stopped after a few feet but heard no movement except his own. He had just begun to entertain the possibility that the monster was gone when he heard the flap of wings again off to his left—and then to his right.

Son of a gun, there are two of them. Two!

He nearly panicked. He was too far from the edge of the field to try and bolt back into the woods, so he lay still, not daring to look up. The beasts crisscrossed the air above the field. They were looking for him, hunting him. The sound of their wings moved to the far end of the field, then back over the woods in the direction from which he'd come. Having no idea where he was, he used the opportunity to slink further out into the field. He slithered around the bales of hay like a snake.

A hiding place. I need a hiding place!

He looked up when he dared. Twice he noticed the creatures above the tree line, silhouetted against the thinning clouds. He could see better now, with the moonlight, but that meant they could too.

His knees and shoulders were sore, and his forearms were cut and bleeding. He didn't think he could crawl much further when he came across a bale of hay that had burst open. The alfalfa had expanded a little and under the bale was a small wash out. He slid down into the shallow. It was not much, but maybe it would be enough. With as little movement as possible, he situated the hay over his body. He felt vulnerable, even though he was sure he couldn't be seen, so he pulled the hay closer, like a blanket, and hunkered deeper. He could feel the sandy dirt below him and the itchy hay above. He prayed that he was covered.

Footsteps! They were on the ground. They were close. He didn't move, he barely breathed. He could sense movement just a few feet away. His heart filled with dread.

They are going to find me! What will they do to me? Kill me? Eat me? Drink my blood? How in the hell did I get in this mess?

He felt the vibrations in the dirt as the footsteps passed. He lay still. Then came the flap of wings. Were they gone? Seconds passed like hours. He wanted to look at his watch, but he didn't dare move. Eventually, he dozed off.

***

He awoke with a start. He was warm. The hay was quite comfortable. He listened. No footsteps, no flap of wings. For a moment he wondered if any of it had really happened. But of course it had. Why else would he be in a field, covered by hay?

My wife! Hours must have passed! My cell!

But what would he say?

Hell, I'll tell her the truth! She can send help!

He slid his hand down to his belt. The phone was gone.

Someone will come. She has probably already called the cops. Surely *there are folks out looking for me.*

Careful not to disturb his cover, he pulled his arm up where he could see his watch. Two o'clock. Dawn was four hours away. He didn't know if these things stayed out past dawn. He didn't even know what they were, but something inside him said that if he made it till dawn, he would be okay.

He heard the flap of wings again, far off, then close, and then far away again. His terror had passed, at least a bit, but he cringed each time he heard them. He fell asleep again and awoke to a gray dawn.

**

He rose cautiously from his hiding place. He didn't know if they were still out there. Did they go in at dawn, wherever the hell 'in' was? What were they? Had he imagined all of it?

In the light of day, he crossed the field and found his way back to the car without much effort. The Ford LTD was a mess. The front end was crushed, and the roof looked like a giant cat had used it for a scratching post. It was not drivable.

He searched the vehicle and located his cell phone, but the battery was dead. "No problem," he mused. He plugged the charger into the cigarette lighter and then into the cell phone. There had to be enough charge left in the car battery to make at least one call, but as he looked down at the screen the 'no service' light appeared.

"Just my damn luck," he grumbled, puzzled because he'd made calls along this stretch before. "Ah, hell." He slammed the car door shut and started down the old gravel road. Home was a good seven miles away, but he figured folks would be out looking for him and he wouldn't have to walk far.

He thought about what he would say. Last night, when the creatures were after him, he would have told the whole story to anyone, the President, the Pope! But now, in the light of day, it all seemed quite silly.

Maybe I just wrecked my rig and hit my head. I probably imagined it all. The roof of the car is *torn, but maybe it got caught under some branches.*

As he walked, the gray clouds overhead seemed to thicken. "Great," he muttered, "now rain."

But the rain held off, and he walked on. There was a small service station and convenience store about two miles up, where the gravel road crossed the paved two-lane highway. He usually took the highway route, but last night he had been running low on gas and the gravel road was a short cut. He knew he could make it before old man Sims closed up for the night. He seldom bought gas there, the price was too high, and he really didn't like the old bastard anyway, but now, as the Shell sign came into view, he knew he'd be glad to see the old fart. As he neared, however, he realized the place was closed.

That's weird. This is Friday morning.

He walked around the store, worried, but found nothing out of the ordinary. When he reached the front again, he stopped at the door. The hours were posted on the glass: 7:30 a.m. to 9:30 p.m., Monday through Saturday, closed Sunday. He looked down at his watch, feeling silly. It was only a quarter to seven.

He breathed a sigh of relief and sat down on the stoop to wait. It was then he realized he was dying of thirst. He bought two Pepsis from the machine by the door and sat back down. He drank both, and waited. 7:30. 8:00. 8:30.

9:00. The old man wasn't coming. And after a while he realized something else—not a single car had passed on the highway. *Something* was wrong.

Home was five miles down the highway and another quarter of a mile down a paved lane. His family was there. There was nothing else for him to do.

Hell, I don't know what's going on, but I am going home, even if I have to walk!

He bought another Pepsi from the machine, downed it quickly, and began to walk.

The highway had been re-paved recently, and the shoulder widened. He'd been pissed every time he'd had to wait while the flag woman held her stop-slow sign, but now he was glad to have the wide shoulder to walk on. Of course, he could have walked down the yellow line, for all the traffic.

Where is everyone? This is no superhighway, but usually there's more traffic than this, even on Sunday— and this is Friday!

Suddenly a thought occurred to him.

Maybe I did hit my head. Maybe I've been out for two days. That must be why the old man didn't show!

He felt of his head, but there was no lump.

Stupid, even if it is Sunday, that doesn't explain the traffic.

He plodded along for a while longer and then finally heard a familiar sound, the roar of an engine coming from up ahead. "A person! A real live person!" he yelled happily, but as the front of the vehicle came into view, his heart sank. A big Dodge power wagon, painted in a green and black camouflage pattern shot past. He kept his eyes to the ground and continued to walk. He heard the screech of brakes and the squeal of tires as the truck did a u-turn and headed back. "Great," he muttered, "just what I need, the local nut."

It was Carl—Crazy Carl, everyone called him. Carl was a survivalist, one of those militia types. He'd been shot up in some conflict in Bosnia or Somalia, hell no one knew which one. None of his neighbors had slept well since he'd moved into the old trailer at the end of the lane. He hadn't actually bothered anyone, but he liked to shoot, a lot, and he'd walled off his place with a tall privacy fence. The roof of his trailer bristled with antennas, and he'd put up a big flag pole with a Confederate flag right out front. There were a lot of 'no trespassing' signs on his fence, along with some more colorful ones like 'If you are found here tonight, you'll be found here tomorrow.' The man was a *nut*.

The big vehicle screeched to a stop, and the passenger door swung open. "Oh hell! Tom! Man, oh man, you're alive, and you haven't been taken!"

"Taken? Taken?" Tom queried, confused.

"Hell, man, where were you last night? Come on, get in!" Carl moved a rather large shotgun off the passenger seat and gestured impatiently. What looked like an Uzi was mounted on the dash, and what appeared to be hand grenades hung from a belt on the shift lever. Tom stared at all the weaponry, alarmed, but Carl patted the seat insistently. "Damn, buddy, come on, get in!"

Tom grimaced and climbed up in the cab. It took some effort since Carl had outfitted the truck with those big mudder tires. "Taken?" he asked again.

"Tom, where were you last night?"

"Well, I was—Carl, have you been by my house? Have you seen my wife, my kids? What *happened* last night?"

"Well, uh, Tom, I… Well, yes, I've been by your house and, um…no one's home. But that's not bad! I mean, well, your car's not there either!"

"Carl, I've got the car—well, it's wrecked. Is the van there?" Carl didn't answer, and Tom could tell by the look on his face that it was. "What has happened?" Tom moaned, dropping his head in his hands.

"Tom, last night we, well, mankind in general, were attacked." He paused, thoughtful, "yeah, I guess that would be the best way to say it. Attacked."

"By what, for heaven's sake?"

"Demons, man!" Carl said, with a fiery look in his eyes. "Well, not exactly demons," he amended in a calmer tone. "I think they're some kind of weird-ass animal. They're killers! Flesh eaters, blood drinkers! But you *can* kill them, that's for damn sure. Hell, I've already got seventeen of them!" He patted the Uzi. "But from what I could get off the internet and the ham radio, this shit is happening all over the world. Sons of bitches ain't gettin' this old boy, you bet your ass! Oh, sorry, Tom I didn't mean to go on like that…"

"Some sort of animal, Carl?" Tom asked, incredulous. "Where did they come from? What do they want?"

"Who knows, Tom?" Carl shrugged. "They want us, that's for sure."

"Are they killing people?"

"Ah…yes. But sometimes they just carry them off! What for, I don't know."

They drove on for a bit, not speaking until they reached their turnoff. Carl's house was at the end of the lane. Tom's was on the left-hand side, and another house sat directly across, on the right side. It belonged to Mr. and Mrs. Evans, a fine old couple. They pulled up into Tom's drive. Tom was out the door and running toward the house before the truck came to a complete stop. The back door was standing open.

"Sue!" he shouted, "Tommy! Karen!" There was no answer. He ran through the house throwing open doors, looking in closets and bathrooms. "Sue! Sue, dammit! Sue!" Despair overwhelmed him. "Sue…oh, Sue!" he broke down, sobbing, "oh no, no…" A hand on his shoulder made him spin, but it was just Carl.

"Perhaps they got away, Tom. I mean, there's no blood or anything."

"The Evans, they will know!" Tom shook off Carl's hand and ran from the house.

"Tom, don't!" Carl yelled from behind him. "Tom, I've—" It was too late. Tom was already across the driveway and running toward the old couple's quaint little house.

The Evans' front door was lying in the front yard. The door facing had been splintered, and slivers of wood filled Tom's palm as he burst through the doorway.

Mr. and Mrs. Evans were dead. Tangled human flesh was strewn about as if it were confetti. Blood splattered the walls, and discarded limbs littered the little front room. Tom stumbled over something, and it rolled. It was Mrs. Evans' head.

"Tom!" He could hear Carl's voice, but it was far away. The room was spinning. He couldn't catch his breath. He felt himself falling, falling forever. Then he felt a thud. He thought it might be himself, but he didn't know. Nor did he care. All went black.

***

Tom awoke to the breathtakingly foul stench of an ammonia tablet being waved under his nose. Carl had dragged him outside onto the grass. "Tom! Tom, you all right? You whacked your noggin pretty damn hard when you went down. It's a hell of a thing, huh Bud?"

"C-Carl? What—who—I mean, what happened?"

"That's what I've been trying to tell you! Some kind of nasty creature has come hunting us!"

Tom sighed and sat up, picking splinters from his hand as he spoke. "Last night, I was driving along the old gravel road when one of them attacked my LTD. It tried to kill me. Then a second one came along! I ran and hid. I got away. Hell, Carl, I thought I was crazy, I didn't know *what* was going on." The terror of the previous night was reflected in his last, desperate question. "What the *hell* is happening?"

"Well, from the best I can tell, Tom, these things have shown up all over the world, Japan, the U.K., the Middle East, Russia, South America, Indonesia, Australia, Europe, *everywhere.* Where they came from and what they are is anybody's guess—there haven't been many news broadcasts since this started. From what I gather, the big cities were hit hardest. The internet is still up, and the electricity is still on, but who knows how long that will last."

"But Sue and the kids, Carl, do you think…?"

Carl placed his hand on Tom's shoulder. "There is a good chance they are still alive. You've seen what kind of mess those monsters leave when they eat."

"Eat?" Tom gasped. "Eat!?"

"Well, yes, they are man-eaters."

"What the hell? What—"

"Hell is right," Carl broke in seriously. "Hell has come to supper, Lad."

"Carl, you said that other places are experiencing the same sort of attacks. The governments, the militaries, what are they doing?"

"Tom, these things came out of nowhere! The military was not really designed to confront something like this. They're fighting, but our bases were not set up for mass guerilla warfare. In places where the citizens are armed—God bless the second amendment—people have fared better, but in places like Japan, China, and other countries where firearm ownership has been outlawed, the populations have been nearly decimated! Here in the good old U.S. things are not quite so bad."

"China," Tom said slowly, "has nearly a *billion* people."

"Not anymore."

"What do they *want,* Carl?"

"Us! For food!" Carl chuckled. "We ain't on the top of the food chain no more."

"This is a nightmare, a *screwed up nightmare.* I just don't believe it!"

"Believe it, Buddy. It's here, it's now and, Tom, it's *real.* Come on, let's go down to my place. I don't know when these bastards will be out again. Maybe they won't come out tonight, who knows?"

"Give me just a minute," Tom said. He walked back over to his house. Inside, he opened a closet door where, high up on a shelf, was his father's World War II Colt 1911. The pistol was old but well oiled, and still worked nicely. It was all he had from his father, who was old when Tom was born and had passed away when he was just two. Tom's mother had raised him by herself, and Tom often wondered if he would have been different had his father lived, tougher, like Ron at work, or like Carl. He set the old .45 on the kitchen table along with an ancient box of shells. He was about to load them into the magazine when Carl walked in.

"That's really nice. I didn't think you owned any firearms. I mean, well, Tom don't take this the wrong way, but you seem like a sissy."

Tom chuckled, and Carl looked surprised. "I am, Carl. I am an out of shape, middle management sissy, who let his family be taken or killed because he was not prepared. I've never been prepared for anything, school, college, work, marriage, fatherhood, nothing! If I'd had a tank full of gas, I might have been home last night instead of getting caught out on that road. Dammit, I hate myself for this!"

Carl held up a hand. "Whoa, Tom, it's not your fault you weren't here! And even if you had been, you don't know what would have happened. You and your whole family might be dead! Here," he offered, as Tom fumbled with the weapon, "let me do that." He took the weapon and squinted down at the bullets in his palm. "Damn, Tom, how old are these?"

"Well, uh…" Tom trailed off, ashamed.

"No matter," Carl said cheerfully. "Come on, I've got a lot of .45 ammo." He patted the pistol on his side as he handed Tom's back. "Besides, you need Hydra-Shoks in this, they will knock the hell out of those lizard lipped sons of bitches. Let's go."

Tom tucked his dad's .45 into his waistband, and they started out the back door. As they passed the fridge, Tom pulled down a small snapshot of Sue and the kids and stuck it in his shirt pocket. They climbed into Carl's truck and drove down the lane to his place. Life had changed, but Tom supposed people all over the world were feeling the same loss.

***

They pulled up to Carl's gate. Carl punched a code on a small keypad, and the gate slid open. Tom couldn't help but gape. Carl had done a lot with the place. It was not at all the full-fledged para-military compound he had anticipated. The paved driveway was lined with neatly tended flower beds. Behind the house was an idyllic garden, complete with a scarecrow. The manicured front lawn was dotted with fruit trees and lawn sculptures, and along the rear fence were poultry pens and rabbit hutches, all neatly covered.

Carl had sided the trailer, added a roof and an addition in the rear. It now resembled a cabin more than the trailer house it had been. Next to the house, Carl had poured a concrete pad and built a garage. Sue and Tom had assumed the concrete trucks meant he was building a bunker.

Carl chuckled at Tom's expression. "Not what you expected, huh?"

"Ah, well…"

"I know. Everybody thinks I'm a survivalist and live in a bunker."

"Well, you know, you *were* shot and then retired. And, well, you do shoot a lot."

Carl laughed. "I was wounded in Bosnia years ago. I retired because my twenty years were up and I shoot a lot because I'm captain of the state pistol team."

They got down from the Dodge and went in. Inside, the house was as much of a shock as the outside. Except for the military memorabilia and the wide variety of guns, the place could have been decorated by Martha Stewart.

"You hungry?" Carl asked, as he set the shotgun in the corner and placed the Uzi in a gun rack near the door.

"No, thanks." Tom's face turned a little green. "I'm still a bit queasy from the Evans."

"Oh, yeah. Look, make yourself at home. I have to check some things."

Carl left the room leaving Tom to look around. A multitude of pictures hung on the wall, Carl and a young, beautiful woman, Carl and the same woman with five children, and Carl in a military uniform. Also, there were several pictures of Carl with some important-looking people. Tom recognized two of them, General Norman Schwarzkopf and former President Clinton.

In the far corner of the room was a uniform in a glass display case, Tom assumed it was Carl's. There were stripes down both arms, and both sides of the chest sported medals. He didn't recognize any of the medals. As a matter of fact, he couldn't even identify what branch of the service the uniform represented. Just then

Carl walked back into the room and saw Tom looking at the case.

"Crazy, huh? You serve?"

"Me? No. My Dad was in World War II, and he was a career military man. He died when I was two and Mom, well, she forbid having anything of that nature around."

"You have your Dad's .45."

"I found it in a box in the attic after Mom died, along with a letter addressed to me that I'd never read."

Carl looked abashed. "Oh, I'm sorry."

"Don't be," Tom chuckled. "Is that your sister or something?" he asked, pointing to the pictures of the woman.

"No," Carl smiled sadly, "that is—was—my wife. She's dead."

"Oh! I'm sorry now."

"No, don't be," Carl said lightly, "it was a while back and I'm okay."

"The kids?"

"Oh, they are alive," he laughed. "Only my wife was killed. The children live with their Grandma and Grandpa in Croatia. See, I married a Croat girl. She was killed while we ate lunch one afternoon in Zagreb. That's Croatia's capital," he explained, at Tom's puzzled look. "It's a beautiful city. My wife was a music professor at the University of Zagreb. In any event, we were eating lunch when a Serbian sniper shot her."

"I'm very sorry, Carl."

Carl looked out across the yard. "Those roses out there were taken from the grounds of the eleventh-century cathedral where she and I were wed, but that was long ago."

"Do you mind if I ask one question, Carl?"

"Sure."

"Why would a sniper want to shoot a music teacher? I mean don't they usually shoot at military people?"

Carl chuckled. "He *was* shooting at a military person. He shot me. The bullet passed through my throat and struck my wife between the eyes. She died in my arms in full view of the cathedral."

"Good lord! Man, I had no idea! It must have been awful. What did you do?"

"Nothing. I had my kids to raise, and I went on. Oh, I healed up, and eventually I went back, hunted down the sniper, killed his wife, his kids, his mother and father— all in front of him, before I cut out his heart. But it did not bring her back..." Carl's voice trailed off, and he had a distant look on his face.

Tom swallowed hard and was wondering what he should say when Carl suddenly snapped back. "Hey, I'm starving. You sure you don't want anything?"

"No thanks."

"Well, okay, let me grab a bite, and we'll get you started."

"Started?"

"Well, yeah, Tom. We've got to get you some ammo, teach you to shoot, and see about finding your wife and children!"

"I can shoot!" Tom eyed Carl defiantly.

"Really, Tom? Well, let me get a bite, and we will see about that."

***

Carl and Tom spent the next week preparing. Their time was split between teaching Tom to shoot and finding out all they could about the creatures. Carl was right about one thing, Tom couldn't shoot, not like Carl.

As best as Tom and Carl could tell the 'gargoyles,' as they dubbed them, were not supernatural. They appeared to be somewhat stronger than most men, but not as strong as some. As the week wore on, they began to see less and less of them—they had learned fast to stay out of the way of Carl's weaponry. They couldn't outmaneuver his bullets, so they just didn't come near. Carl and Tom dissected one who came too close and determined they were some kind of animal. They had hearts, livers, lungs, and red blood. While they were somewhat different, they were not alien.

"They are just a damn animal," Carl spat in disgust, after they finished the dissection.

"Like us," Tom mused.

"No, Tom, God put *us* in charge. Never forget that." Tom had never thought of Carl as a religious man.

76

On two evenings they went out 'hunting,' as Carl called it. Traveling should have been difficult since martial law had been declared, but Carl knew many of the soldiers they encountered and, quite frankly, the soldiers were glad to see some folks out helping. On their second night out—the gargoyles seemed to come out only at night—Carl shot one down. It was wounded and made odd grunting sounds as Carl moved in to finish it off. Tom and Carl stared dispassionately down at it, then Carl raised his big .454 Causal and pulled back the hammer.

"Wait," the beast said.

You could have knocked Carl and Tom over with a feather. "It talks!" Carl said.

"Don't kill me." The thing's voice was low and guttural, but clear.

"And why not?" Carl growled.

"I can help you."

"Help us with what?"

"Help you find *his* family." It pointed a leathery finger at Tom.

"You son of a bitch!" Tom sputtered.

Carl pushed his pistol against the thing's chin and looking it straight in the eyes. "You'd better start talking. *Now.*"

So the beast began a tale, mythical and fantastic and, ultimately, evil.

"We are what your ancient legends call Watchers."

"That's just a myth," Tom scoffed.

"Most legends are based in fact," Carl said without looking away. "I know. I spent a lot of time in the old world. Just because we do not believe it anymore, does not make it go away."

"We, the Watchers, existed before man. We ruled the earth millennia ago, but *He* chose to create you. For a while, our races existed in relative harmony, but then, as you multiplied you demanded more resources, more space. There were wars. We were hunted, killed, and finally, *He* banished us to another realm, another dimension, as you call it. There we regrouped, multiplied, and ultimately flourished." The beast shook its fist proudly but dropped it quickly as Carl shoved the pistol harder against its face. "Our new world was a gentler place, there were no men to hunt us. And our prophets told us that someday the door separating the two worlds would open and we could return. Seven days ago that day came."

"But if the new world was so grand, why return here?" Carl asked.

"This was our home. We were here first."

Carl looked puzzled. "I have a few more questions—"

Tom held up his hand. "Wait, how do you know my family was taken?"

"I took them—the same night I hunted you." Tom raised his Dad's old .45 and jerked the slide back. "Wait, wait, they live! They, along with many others, are being held at, uh, a central location. There are many such holding facilities all around the world. They are not being harmed."

"What about the Evans?" Carl snarled.

The beast did not answer, but instead looked at Carl and said, "if you will give your word to release me without harm, I will tell you our secret." Carl looked up at Tom, who nodded.

Carl smiled maliciously. "Okay, I will not harm you."

So the beast continued his story. "While the other world was more gentle, there was one thing absent. Man."

"But I thought you hated us," Carl said.

"Hate you?" The beast's lips parted in a ghastly grin. "We *love* your flesh, your blood. It nourishes us in ways you cannot imagine. So, from the beginning of our banishment, we chose the strongest of our race to come back, to invade."

"So you are holding my family and the others for *food?*"

"Well, not all of them. We are not so different from you. Your women are much like ours and, quite frankly, we prefer them."

"So, you are going to *rape* our wives and *eat* our children?" Tom growled, horrified.

"Not rape," the gargoyle scoffed. "We can pleasure your women in ways you cannot. They like it!" His lumpy face twisted in a smirk. "In fact, it was your *wife* who told me where to find you that night."

"Where is my family being held?"

"About thirty miles from here, but *you* will never get in."

"You said a door opened. What do you mean by that?" Carl asked.

"Ah, yes. Well, from time to time a portal opens between our worlds. There is more than one door, but they are never open for long, and it is never known when they will open. For thousands of years, each time one opened, a few of my kind would go through. We never heard from them again."

"So what changed?" Tom queried.

"Some of your people are disgusted with the way you treat God's creation. They wish to give it back to those who were in charge first, those who can and *will* be better stewards of the planet. You see, we don't need cars," it twitched its leathery wings and winced. There was a jagged tear in one wing made by a bullet from Carl's gun. "For a promise to allow them to live and retain control of a portion of the world, we agreed to decrease your surplus population and return our mother world to its former wild and glorious state."

Carl's finger stroked the trigger. "Who are these traitors to mankind?" he growled.

"You promised not to kill me, remember?" the beast said nonchalantly. Carl lowered his pistol, and the beast continued.

"There are groups of you who oppose the cutting down of trees, the killing of animals, the other atrocities you have brought on this world."

"So let me get this straight," Tom said, "you don't mind wiping us out, slaughtering our kind, but don't cut down a *tree?*"

"These friends we have are in the highest places."

"The White House?" Carl asked.

"Not that high," the gargoyle conceded, "but in what you call Congress. You see, right now the gates are fixed, stationary. Our friends, those of your race who see the truth, hold open the door with your so-called science, and we come through. Soon we all will be here. Two weeks, one month and all my people will be together."

"People?" Tom barked a laugh. "*We* are the people. You are a damn flying iguana that just happens to talk. And my wife would never submit to the likes of you!"

"Hold on, Tom," Carl said, holding his hand out toward Tom, and addressed the gargoyle again. "How is it you know all this?"

"I am a High Commander."

"There have been attacks all over the world," Tom argued. "How is that possible with help from only from our country?"

"Our friends' connections transcend your kind's fleeting political boundaries."

"You speak English very well," Carl observed.

"Some of us do, and some don't," the creature answered smugly.

"Do you know the names of those who helped you?"

"Even if I did, I would never tell you—even if you went back on your word and killed me. Besides," it sat up gingerly, "I've told you enough. I can get back before daylight if I leave now, though my second failure to kill you will likely lead to my demotion."

"One more question," Carl said quickly. "Why can't you come out in daylight?"

"Very well," it sighed. "We could, long ago, but the world we were banished to is different from this. The light is different, diffused. Daylight here burns us, but our friends, your scientists, say we will acclimate. We have been gone these six thousand years. The old ones died, and new generations were born. You see, we have no science, no writing. We hand all traditions down orally, from generation to generation. We do not pollute ourselves with what you call technology."

Righteous indignation welled up in Tom and the anger he had tried to contain hardened into a cold rage. He smiled—a long, slow, menacing movement. "I was raised a widow's son. This thing," he waved his gun, "is one of two things I have from my Dad. This is some of our technology. It is neither good nor bad, it is just a hunk of steel."

"Stolen from the earth," the beast snapped.

"Mined is the word we use," Tom continued, undeterred. "The bullets in it are called hydroshocks, I am told. You see, I did not know about this sort of stuff until a week ago when *you* forced me to learn." Tom leveled the gun at the beast's head.

"You liar. You promised. Mankind is all alike, traitorous, deceitful truce breakers."

"First of all, *you* declared war on *us,* and second, the terms were that he," Tom pointed at Carl, "would not kill you." Tom pulled the trigger and the .45 bucked in his hand. The hydroshock slug took the gargoyle square between the eyes. It flailed for a bit and then lay still, dead.

"Damn, Tom," Carl chuckled. "You're turning into a hard ass."

"I ain't even started yet."

Carl and Tom drove on back to Carl's house. Tom felt a melancholy pang as they passed by his home. The darkened windows should have been lit with life and love.

Carl looked over at Tom as they pulled through the gate. "You know what you have to do?"

"Yes," he said slowly. "We have to go and get my family."

"You have to," Carl corrected. "I have to stay here."

"But you are the war hero! I *need* you!"

"Tom, look at me. Look around you. See all these antenna's, these microwave dishes? Tom, I was a communications expert in the Army. I can shoot this whole thing down. I can *stop* it. I know the people who know the people behind this."

"Like your buddy, Bill Clinton?" Tom jeered.

"Hell, Tom, that's just a cardboard cut out. I would never have supported his policies."

"Really?"

"Really," he replied. "It was a joke in my army unit." He straightened proudly. "Stormin' Norman, now *that* one is real."

"But how did you get shot as a communications expert? And how did you get all those medals? How did you learn to shoot like that?"

"It's a long story, Tom, but let's just say I was not always a communications technician." He patted Tom on the shoulder as they walked toward the house. "Now lad, you've got work to do."

***

Carl made some calls. He explained the situation to some of his Army friends, and they agreed to storm the compound. Though he remained behind, Carl loaned Tom a good number of weapons to see him through.

The compound was guarded by both men and beasts. Carl and the soldiers with him killed both equally. It was a tough battle, but Tom finally located Sue deep within.

"Sue!" he shouted as he ran toward his lovely wife. "Thank goodness I've found you. Oh, baby, I'm so sorry!"

"Tom!" she gasped. "What are you doing here? What are you doing with those guns? Tom, you're not a gun nut. Tom, what are you *doing?*"

"Come on, Sue," he said impatiently and grabbed her arm, "I'll tell you about it later.

We've got to get out of here! The kids, Sue, where are the kids?"

"Oh, the kids are fine, just fine. Tommy Junior is working in the kitchens and Karen is in the other room." Sue shook off Tom's hand and pointed to a door.

"Tommy, working?"

"He is thirteen, Tom—"

"Sue, are you okay?"

"—and Karen is fourteen, Tom, you know, old enough for…"

"Sue, what the hell? Have you been drugged or something? Let's get the kids and get the hell out!"

"No!" Sue shrieked, slamming her fists into his face. "Damn you, Tom, damn you to hell! I'm not going and my children are not going either! I've found love, *true love*. We are staying!"

Tom had seen many horrible things since the invasion began, but Sue's reaction was by far the most shocking. "Sue, what are you saying?" he groaned. Just then the door burst open and one of the gargoyles stepped through. His hands were wrapped around the neck of Tom's fourteen-year-old daughter and he was using her for a shield.

He spoke, his voice dripping with condescension. "What she's saying, *Tom*, is she doesn't want to go. She likes me more than you."

"Look, you bastard, I don't know what you have done to my wife but I—"

"Your wife! Ha, ha, ha." His wretched laughter rang mockingly in Tom's ears. "She is mine now. She belongs to me and your she-child will be mine too, soon. Soon she will submit to me." His hand played around the corner of Karen's mouth. Pure terror showed in her eyes. Then she bit him, hard, right on his scaly finger. The beast screamed in agony and flung her across the room.

Tom's old .45 seemed to have a life of its own as it bucked in his hand. He worked the trigger repeatedly, feverishly. The first slug took the beast in the shoulder, the second in the thigh and the third, squarely in the stomach. It collapsed on the floor and Sue ran to its side.

"Oh darling! Oh no! Tom, you *bastard.* You no good, rotten bastard! What have you done?" She fell next to the dying beast, weeping. "Oh no...no..."

Ignoring Sue, Tom knelt next to Karen, fearing the worst, but she opened her eyes and wrapped her arms around his neck in a tight hug.

"Daddy," she wept, "oh gosh, Daddy, it was awful! They wanted me to..." Tears streamed from her eyes and sobs wracked her body. "They said they would kill me, eat me! But Daddy, I knew you would come! Mom said you were dead, but I *knew.*"

"It's okay, baby," Tom said soothingly. "Come on. Let's go." He picked Karen up off the floor. "Sue?" he called. "Sue? Susan! Come on, let's go home."

"Go to hell, you bastard," she snapped venomously. Then she spit at him. "You can go straight to hell."

Tom looked down at the dying gargoyle. Dark blood oozed from his wounds and when he coughed, his chin was covered with pink foam. "We will prevail," it grimaced. "We will take back what was ours. Never forget it!"

"You forgot the most important thing," Tom replied, "something I have just begun to realize. *He* left us in charge and while we may not be the best, God is sovereign. He does what He wants, and what He wants is us."

"It was our tradition first."

"We have an old tradition here." Tom smiled. "We shoot men who sleep with our wives." The Colt spoke again and a nice, neat hole appeared between the gargoyle's eyes. He slumped over, dead, and Susan wailed louder.

"Let's go, Karen. We have to find your brother." Tom turned his back on Susan, leaving her to mourn her adulterous lizard lover.

***

Six months passed. Carl was true to his word and the entire conspiracy had been revealed. Most of the humans responsible were rounded up and publicly executed—no due process, just justice. Clean up of all the beasts was still under way and things were slowly beginning to return to normal—with a few exceptions. Most people wore or carried guns and, in countries where there were enough people left to be tense, international tensions had been relieved.

"You know, it's funny," Carl observed one day, as they rose from the dinner table, "how a common enemy can unite man."

"It sure did," Tom agreed.

"How are you holding up, Tom?"

"You know, Carl, it's like a great man once told me. I've got my kids to raise and killing won't bring her back." Carl's face reddened. "You know, Carl," Tom smiled, "I probably should get out and try to meet a few single women."

Carl laughed. "Well, old pal, you think those lizards are mean!"

The End

JUST BELIEVE

Sam turned his key in the lock. He had, in fact, turned the same key in the same lock five nights a week for the past year and a half. It was second nature to him now. Each night, in the dark, he would run his fingers across the ten or so keys on the ring and his sense of touch would alert him to the familiar shape that gained him access to his place of employment. Tonight, however, the keys felt different. Sam even went so far as to remove his flashlight from the ring on his duty belt to ensure he had indeed brought the proper set.

His furrowed his brow as he jiggled the key in the lock. It almost felt as though someone held the knob from the other side, but after a moment it turned smoothly, just as it always had in the past. Sam propped the door open with his foot and checked the lock several times from both sides. Frowning, he made a mental note to inform the maintenance person something was wrong. But what would he say? It felt funny?

It must be the weather, he thought. An early cold front had come through and there was probably a bit of ice in the tumbler. He dismissed the incident from his mind as he disarmed the alarm.

The Powder River Knife Works had a sophisticated alarm system but the management felt having an armed security officer on the property at night was a better insurance policy. That set well with Sam. He truly enjoyed his job at the Knife Works, one of the largest knife warehouses in the country—maybe the world. Knives of every genre were on display in the spectacular showroom, along with a plethora of other weapons, antiques and memorabilia, and Sam never got tired of examining all the various items.

He let the door swing closed, shutting out the dim light from the parking lot. As he felt along the wall for the light switch, a sudden cold fell hard upon his hand. It was so disturbing to him that he drew back for a moment before switching on the lights. But as the hall lights came on, a familiar sense of place settled over him and he began to think he was acting quite silly.

First the lock and now this. Ridiculous.

Sam padded down the hallway to his office. The key slid into the lock and he opened the door without incident. He shared the office with his relief man, Clifford, who seldom used it and who was careful never to disturb anything when he did. Sam had never said anything, never given Clifford any indication he did not want him there, but everyone, not just Cliff, knew the office was Sam's domain. Housekeeping never entered, nor did maintenance. If the trash needed emptied, Sam did it himself. If anything needed fixed, he repaired it himself. For well over a year now the office had been exclusively his territory. That is why he thought it strange to see the picture lying on the floor, the glass shattered.

A distinct scowl crossed his weathered face as he surveyed the damage. The picture was of himself shaking hands with President Bush. 'The Gold Coast will always be much safer with men like Sam Priest on the job,' the inscription read, and it was signed, 'Your Buddy, George Bush.' Sam had been the head of a drug task force that netted the largest bust of cocaine ever. The president had awarded Sam a particularly high honor by visiting him personally.

The bust had actually landed Sam an early retirement—after six months in the hospital recovering from the four 9mm bullets he took in the back. He was lucky, though, he had walked away. Two other officers hadn't. With the love of his family for help, Sam was up and about in less than a year, with a gold watch and a pension to follow.

"Well, shit. I guess I'll have to get another frame." He pulled the picture free from the debris and set it on his desk, then used a broom and dustpan to clean up the glass. He glanced over the rest of the room but nothing else had been disturbed. The north wall of the room was an outside wall. Perhaps a truck had hit it while unloading and jarred the picture. Sam wrote his arrival time on the shift log and left the office to begin his rounds.

He had just closed the office door when he heard the echo of laughter. It was a deranged sound, bouncing through several octaves before cutting off abruptly. A cold chill ran down his spine, and he eased out his 9mm auto.

No one was supposed to be in the building. Hell, no one *could* be in the building, he had shut down the alarm himself. If anyone had been in the building when he got there, they would have set off the motion sensors and sounded the alarm. However, in spite of all that, Sam was sure of what he'd heard.

He slipped down the hall, gun ready, easing toward the sound. The laughter sounded again, louder, as Sam neared the showroom. *They won't be laughing in a minute,* he thought grimly. Holding the 9mm close to his chest, he reached for the knob. With a twist of the wrist, he would be back in the world of confrontation. Two steps more and he would be face to face with that same old feeling, the knowing that you have a second to decide, but a lifetime to live with that decision.

Sam turned the knob slowly, then threw open the door and burst into the showroom. The door bounced off the wall with a bang, and the laughter stopped as suddenly as it began. "Freeze!" Sam yelled, as he cleared the door facing and entered the big room, but he was alone.

He moved through the entire area, looking behind displays and under tables, but he was all by himself. *I am losing it,* he thought, as he holstered his gun in disgust.

Sam had always been a reasonable man. "Everything has a logical explanation," he had said a thousand times. But he had heard stories that the Knife Works was haunted because it was built on an old Indian burial site.

"Really!" one of the clerks had assured him. "She is a beautiful Indian Princess!"

"Haha," Sam had laughed, "and I bet her name is Spookahantas! Hahaha."

The red-faced clerk had hurried off, but not before issuing Sam a strong warning. "You had better watch your tongue!"

As Sam recalled that conversation, another thought occurred to him and his face grew flushed. Someone on the day shift must be playing a joke on him. Well, Sam did not believe in spooks, now or then, and he knew how to get to the bottom of this.

He left the showroom. At the end of the hall was the video surveillance room. If anyone was in the building, Sam would find out who, and where. *I'll get you now,* he thought, as he sat down in front of the monitors. *We'll see just what's up.*

He spent several minutes flipping through the files, but an hour of fast reverse only showed him what he had already suspected he'd find. No one had been in the showroom. Sam reset the camera and resumed the current scan of the showroom. It was still clear.

Well, enough of this, he thought, *I need to start my rounds.* He started to stand up when the laughter began again. This time it was closer and louder. As a matter of fact, it sounded like it was right outside the door. Sam flipped the monitor to the hallway camera and turned it manually so he could see the other side of the door. There was nothing there.

Sam drew his weapon. Enough was enough. If this was a joke, it had gone too far, and someone was about to get hurt. He burst through the door, gun in hand. Only his quick reflexes saved him from plowing head-on into the man who stood a few feet from the door. Sam twisted sideways and turned as he drew his weapon up. The man was about six feet tall, slightly built, around one hundred and sixty pounds. He had dark hair, brown eyes, and wore ceremonial Indian dress. In his right hand, he held a large war club. Sam's well-trained eyes took all this in as he landed flat on his back a few feet away. Years of training, and innate instincts that training could never match, kept the gun aimed right at the man who stood before him.

"Do not move!" Sam snapped from his position on the floor. He eased himself up on one knee and then the other, carefully keeping the gun trained on the man. The man stood motionless. "Put the club down! Now!" The uninvited guest just stood there, his brazen stare fixed right on Sam. "Drop it! Now!" Sam ordered again.

Still, the Indian did not move. "What in the hell is a matter with you?" Sam finally asked. At that, the Indian began to move, slowly, and Sam breathed a sigh of relief. But to Sam's dismay, instead of placing the club on the floor, the man raised it high above his head and with a scream that would follow Sam for the rest of his life, the outlandish apparition rushed headlong toward him. Sam squeezed off two rounds, and in a fraction of a second it was all over. Both shots took the Indian squarely in the beaded breastplate of his authentic looking costume, and he reeled back a few steps in disbelief. The sound of the gunshots was still echoing down the hall as the Indian met Sam's gaze. For an instant the Indian's eyes were red with fire, warrior's eyes, and then he was gone. Not dead, but vanished into thin air. Gone.

Sam stood still for several moments, his eyes fixed on where the man had just been. There was nothing there now except a single small feather floating slowly to the floor. Finally, he shook his head and eased himself into a nearby chair. Without a doubt, he had just gone over the edge.

After he sat for what seemed like hours, he rose from the chair. There were reports to write and people to call. What would he say? Too many years of intense stress had taken their toll. *I have finally cracked. But why now, dear Lord? Why not back then?*

Puzzled, and in no hurry to call anyone and admit his madness, Sam inspected the wall behind where the Indian had stood. There were no bullet holes. He emptied the magazine and counted his shells. Two were missing. He looked down and sure enough, two spent casings lay on the floor a few feet away. He had fired those shots, and they had hit something, but what?

"Where in the blazes did you go?" he shouted in frustration.

A low chuckle answered his question. He spun on one heel to find the Indian had returned, and this time he wasn't alone. A few feet behind the first man stood another man, younger, also dressed as an Indian. This one held a bow and arrow, aimed right at Sam.

Sam's eyes widened. *This is not happening,* he thought, as he heard the twang of the bowstring. Fortunately for Sam, his Kevlar vest was equipped with a trauma plate, a half-inch thick plate of solid tungsten steel. He felt the impact and staggered a little from the blow, but the arrow plunked harmlessly to the ground. Before it could register in Sam's brain that the arrows were indeed real, the young brave let go with another. The second arrow grazed Sam's left arm, tearing his uniform shirt and leaving a deep scratch in his skin. The tickle of blood trickling down the outside of his arm snapped Sam back to reality. These guys were real!

Sam tucked and rolled, and a third arrow sank deep into the wall-board where his head had been a second before. He reared up and fired a two-round burst at the young brave. This time the Indian didn't disappear, he just gave a maniacal laugh and ran off down the hall with the older warrior close behind. Sam heard a door slam and the laughter cut off. They were in the showroom.

On the floor a few feet away from Sam lay three arrows. He squatted and picked one up. It was not a modern arrow, not aluminum or even turned wood. It appeared homemade. Though the shaft was straight, there were nicks in it from a knife, and the fletchings were real feathers. When Sam realized the red stuff on the tip was his blood, he grimaced and dropped it. He stood up and replaced the partially used clip in his gun with a fresh one from the holder on his belt, carefully tucking the partial clip in its place. *Eighteen rounds ready again,* he thought, as he pulled back the slide and gave pursuit.

He didn't have far to go. Less than twenty feet inside the showroom door stood the two warriors, ready and waiting. Sam ducked behind a glass display case and came up firing. Six rounds apiece, center mass—six rounds that would have killed anyone else on the planet—had no effect on Sam's two adversaries. They merely threw their heads back, laughing, and ran off into the darkened showroom.

Sam slid in behind a massive display case and began to assess his situation. The Rangers had taught him some valuable lessons in Vietnam, one of which he always used when he had a problem. The first step was to identify the problem. *Okay, Two specters from beyond the grave are trying to kill me. They are apparently impervious to bullets.* The second step was to select a plan of action. *I can't kill whatever it is so it's time to get the heck out of Dodge.* The final step was to initiate the plan.

Sam Priest was afraid of no one, he was no coward, but it was obviously time to go. He chose the quickest route to the door and began to make his way there, slipping behind display cases and watching carefully for movement. He passed by a rugged looking display case made of rough-hewn log. In the case was a club similar to the one the Indian wielded. Previously Sam had paid little attention to this case, but now, in the face of death, he couldn't take his eyes from it.

Mounted at the top of the display was a model 76 Winchester lever action rifle. Displayed below the rifle was a cracked and worn photograph, and next to that was a yellowed news clipping with the headline 'Last Two Renegades Taken by Authorities.' The picture showed a rugged looking frontier man holding the same model 76. Two dead men were laid out in front of him. As Sam looked closely at their faces, he was, for the first time in his life, truly scared. Without a doubt, these were the same two men he had just shot. He stared closer at the picture. The landscape behind the frontier man looked eerily familiar, but there was no way he had ever seen it. Even the face of the rugged mountaineer tugged at his memory.

How can this be? Sam thought. *Two dead Indians come back from the Great Beyond to kill me? What have I ever done to them?*

Just then he heard the crash of a display case being knocked over followed by the sound of taunting laughter. He knew the men wouldn't give him much more time. He would have to decide quickly what he was going to do.

For many years Sam had insisted he didn't believe in ghosts, but deep inside he did believe. He had seen one. Years ago, shortly after his Granny died, Sam saw her walking through the grape arbor in his back yard. When he approached her, she smiled and said one thing before she faded away. "Sammy," she said, "just believe."

Well, by gosh, he believed now. He had a six-inch gash on his arm to help him.

A slight breeze brushed the back of his neck—not the cold chill he had felt before, but a warm, summer-like touch—and the smell of honeysuckle tickled his nose. "Sammy, just believe," a voice whispered behind him. Sam spun around, gun leveled, but there was no one there.

"Granny." The word slipped through in a whisper. He knew what he had to do.

Sam turned back to the display case. Raising his gun high above it, he brought the butt down hard. The antique glass shattered into long shards and stagnant air rushed up to meet his flaring nostrils. He reached carefully past the jagged glass and removed the old Winchester. The weapon had a familiar feel to it. As he ran his fingers down the stock, he knew instinctively where he would feel a nick or a dent. In the case next to the picture lay a box of 44/40s. He loaded the gun quickly and muttered, "I hope you still work." As he slipped the extra shells in his pocket, he felt at ease, as though the weight on his shoulders, though not lifted, had lightened.

Just then he saw a white blur out of the corner of his eye. He turned, and an arrow sank into the wood of the case. The two were moving back toward him.

"Well, here goes!" Sam shouted. "This gun killed you once, it will do it again!" Before sprinting away from the case, he reached in for one last thing. He removed the picture from its resting place and turned it over. The writing on the back was no real surprise. In bold print were the words 'Sam P., Mountain Man, kilt two fugitive Injuns. Dec. 23, 1862. Missoula, Montana Territory'.

He smiled. "Just believe."

Sam peered around the side of another display case in time to see the older Indian slip behind a giant stuffed grizzly bear. A clear shot would be out of the question without a better position, and he had lost track of the other man. He slid out a little further to try to get a better view. A split second later the table of Kabar knives beside him flipped into the air and came crashing down behind him.

The young brave stood and slashed at Sam with a big Bowie knife. The blade missed Sam's throat by less than an inch as the brave's arm swung in a wild arc. Off balance from the missed blow, the brave stumbled into Sam. Sam brought the toe of his well-shined Wellington up into the brave's belly, and the Indian sank to the floor. Before the young brave had a chance to recover, Sam slammed the butt of the Winchester across his cheek. Bright red blood splattered over Sam's pristine uniform as a large gash opened along the Indian's cheek bone, running nearly from nose to ear. *The gun hurt him,* Sam thought with a thrill, *I was right!*

The older brave had used the distraction to close in on Sam. As the injured brave tucked and rolled behind a group of boxes, Sam parried a blow from the wicked looking war club and sidestepped the older Indian. Flipping the rifle in the air, Sam grabbed it by the barrel. He swung it wide and brought the butt down square on the older warrior's back. The war club slipped from the brave's fingers as he fell to his knees. Sam flipped the rifle back into shooting position. "Just believe," he said savagely, as he jacked a shell into the chamber. The older warrior had regained his feet. He held the club high over his head, but Sam leveled the gun at his chest. *Aim and fire,* Sam thought calmly, but he caught a movement out of the corner of his eye. The young Indian had drawn his bow and arrow again.

Sam ducked sideways, and the arrow that would have taken him in the throat just grazed his collar. As he ducked, his finger jerked the trigger of the big saddle gun. A resounding boom filled the room as the 40-caliber bullet tore through the leg of the older warrior. The warrior screamed and fell to the floor.

Sam didn't waste any time. He spun on one heel and with a practiced motion, jacked a second slug into the big Winchester. The brave was notching his last arrow when Sam raised the rifle again. The young brave hardly seemed to notice the blast. His eyes narrowed for a just a second, and a puzzled expression crossed his face, then he dropped the bow, took two steps backward and fell against the far wall, dead from the single bullet hole square between his eyes.

Sam turned back to see the older brave had somehow gotten to his feet and was hobbling out the door. Sam reached the hallway just in time to see the Indian stagger outside. Sam followed him out, just seconds behind.

As Sam stepped out the door, he saw the Indian on the ground, tangled up with a uniform that looked just like Sam's. "My word," Sam whispered, as he finally realized what had happened, "is it already time for my relief? Have I been chasing them that long?" But there was no mistaking it, the man on the ground with the wild Indian was none other than Clifford, and when the Indian came up on top, he had none other than Clifford's gun.

"Oh dear lord, no!" Clifford shouted as he grabbed at the man's arm. Cliff carried a Smith and Wesson .44

magnum revolver. The oversized pistol kicked wildly as the Indian fired. The bullet struck with a spark on the sidewalk just a few inches from Cliff's head. The Indian brought the pistol down to try again, but he was too late.

Sam fired from the hip—at that range, there was no need to aim. He worked the lever so quickly that Cliff would later swear he only heard one long round go off, but there were, indeed, two. The first round took the Indian square in the throat. The second hit him in the chest. Sam's eyes met the warrior's for the second time, but this time he saw only surprise. A long second passed, and then the warrior's eyes glazed over, and he fell backward onto the concrete sidewalk, dead.

***

The blue lights had finally gone. Inside, the staff were cleaning up. Alone in the parking lot, Sam stared across the valley floor to the low mountains beyond. The Winchester rifle lay on the hood of his truck. It was funny, but no one had even asked to see it. Sam quirked a smile at the thought and then set the rifle on the seat of his pickup. He started to climb in when an oversized hand fell upon his shoulder. It was Cliff.

"Hey, Buddy, the Captain figures those guys were crazies escaped from the loony bin over at Morristown. He said they may never be able to I.D. them for sure." He squinted into the cab. "Say, where'd you get that rifle?"

Sam grinned. "I've had it for years. More than a hundred, I guess."

Clifford chuckled. "Yeah, you're the last of the great Indian fighters. Ha, ha, ha." His voice cracked, and his lower lip quivered. "You saved my life, Sam." Tears welled up in the big man's eyes.

"Hell, weren't nothing," Sam said. He smiled as he removed his badge and handed it to Cliff.

"What's this?" Cliff asked.

"I quit."

"But... Uh, where will you go?"

"Montana," Sam said, as he slid into the truck.

"Montana?" Clifford scratched his head.

"Yep," Sam said. He turned the key and Clifford raised his voice to be heard over the sound of the engine.

"I can't believe it!"

"You should!" Sam shouted back as he pulled away. "Just believe!"

Clifford watched until the truck faded from view. As he turned to go inside, on the breeze, he could hear the faintest whisper. "Just believe."

The End

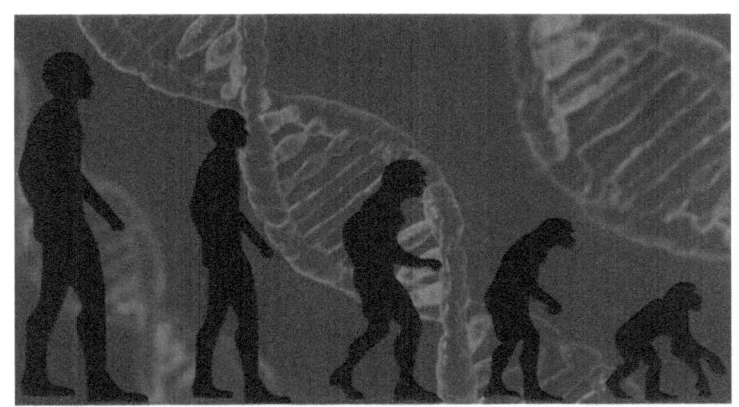

BETTER

The man-beast perched on the limb, his chest muscles straining against the shredded remains of his shirt. Soon these last fragments of humanity would fall away, and he would be just a beast.

Once he had been just a man. Puny. Pathetic. Now he was stronger. Faster. Better.

The night air burned his nostrils as he sucked it in. On the air was the sweet scent of flesh and blood. Man's flesh. The man-beast was a manhunter—no other flesh would sustain him. And the more he partook, the further he slipped into the beast. Very soon the thoughts of man, the trappings of man would be gone. He would be wild. Better.

The Prometheus implant was deceptively simple. Once implanted it emitted minute electrical impulses that hyper-stimulated the parts of the brain that control strength, intellect, sexual pleasure and enjoyment of food, among other things. Once implanted, it was impossible to remove. And at first, no one wanted it removed. Hell, you were superhuman! Better!

Unfortunately, there were unforeseen complications.

The man-beast remembered the euphoria he felt when he first received his implant, his new found strength and, of course, the endless hours of sex. He remembered a mate. His altered mind struggled for the word...wife. Yes...he had a wife... He could not recall what had become of her.

But science had not foreseen what was to come. Hormones and proteins were used up faster than the body could replace them. Even supplements failed to keep up with the body's new demands. After a few months, the superhuman traits gave way to regression in some areas. First to go were societal inhibitions and morality. Finally, each person who received the implant succumbed to a complete breakdown, descending into a psychosis from which they never recovered. Strength and sexual prowess remained, yet those with the implant were still only as strong as the limits of their human bodies allowed. And the only way to replace the necessary proteins was to feed on the only flesh that contained them.

The man-beast had watched as much of the population regressed. He had held out longer than most, but yes...he did remember...his wife. He had killed her, devoured her...and...his offspring. A tug of sorrow pulled at him, but it was nothing more than the ghost of feelings he had once known.

He drew the night air in again. The man, his prey, was closer. Soon he would feast. Sometimes, during the daylight, when he lay curled in whatever den he had chosen, the bloodlust would fade, but the return of the darkness always renewed his need. He hated man, but he loved the flesh, the blood...

He licked his lips as the scent of man passed through his nostrils. His prey was nearly beneath him now. He could barely hold back. He inhaled quietly and detected another scent—a second human. His lips peeled away from his teeth in a silent snarl. Better than one man, now he would have two.

Even as he readied himself to attack, a third scent filled his nostrils. It was dog. Dogs hunted the beast. They hated the beast as much as the beast hated man. The beast drew in on himself, near to panic. He could hear the dogs' breathing, their panting and slobbering excitement growing nearer. Where seconds before the beast had been the hunter, now he was the hunted, the frightened prey hiding in the forest.

He started to move, then froze. The first man had come too close. Caught off guard by the presence of the dogs, the beast was cornered. Adrenalin surged through his body as scent and sound revealed he was surrounded by dogs. His only chance of escape lay past the first man. He would not have time to eat, but he would certainly kill the man.

He rose up on the limb to jump, tearing away the last shreds of his shirt. As he looked down something seemed vaguely familiar about this particular man. The dogs closed in, snapping and pulling at their leashes. With an eerily human yell, the trapped beast leaped.

Blinding white light flashed. Something struck the beast. He hit the ground on his knees. Sharp pain shot through his legs and was gone, but the spasms radiating from his stomach doubled him over and refused to dissipate. He struggled to his feet. He was very tired. The hounds were almost upon him, but the beast no longer cared. Escape now his only concern, he tried to run. A second blinding flash erupted, and darkness descended.

***

The man holstered his magnum and gazed down sadly at the carcass that was once the husband of his baby sister. The beast's features were twisted almost beyond recognition, but the man knew who he was. Another man walked up cradling a rifle in the crook of his arm.

"Big John, you got him, huh?"

"Yes. Yes, I did." Surprisingly soft-spoken for his size, Big John was dressed in dark clothing and a tan hunting vest. "Billy, I hate this."

"I know, John." Billy was a small man, but his confidence and capability made him a comforting presence during this crisis. He reached up and patted John's shoulder. "I know, buddy, but now he's gone. He can't hurt anyone else. Come on, we have a lot more hunting to do tonight." Billy walked purposefully into the darkness.

John kicked the carcass. "How could you?" he whispered. "I told her not to stay with you, but she loved you. And you ate her and your own children! How could you?"

Billy's voice crackled over the two-way radio on John's belt. "John! John, we may have another one! We need you!"

"I hope you're better now," John whispered. Then he walked away.

***

Unseen by the men, a wraith watched. Freed, now, from his twisted body, he could remember and regret the atrocities he had committed. All he had really wanted was to be better. He looked longingly after his brother-in-law. They had once been friends.

The wraith felt a tugging, as though a breeze was flowing through him, pulling him away. He turned from his carcass toward a light.

To his dismay, though not to his surprise, he found not the soft, welcoming light of eternal peace, but the harsh revealing light of eternal judgment.

The End

Special thanks to Aphelion Ezine for the first publication of this story in 2005 as New and Improved.

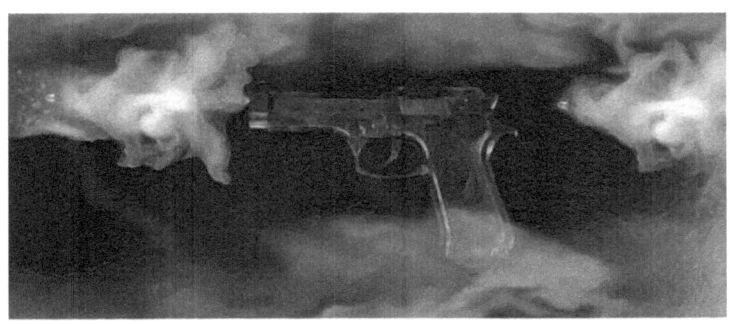

FULL CIRCLE

Daniel looked carefully up and down the road before opening the trunk. When he was sure no one was around, he lifted the lid and flipped up the false bottom. The hollow had once held a spare tire but was now fitted with the tools of Daniel's trade.

From the assorted items in front of him, Daniel selected a twenty-two caliber semiautomatic pistol. The weapon held fourteen rounds in an extended magazine. It had no front sight. Instead, the end of the barrel was threaded to fit a silencer, and a laser sight was employed to ensure accuracy.

Other items in the hidden compartment included a sawed-off twelve gauge shotgun, a snub nose .357 and a twenty-two rifle with a Leupold scope. With the rifle, Daniel could shoot a gnat off a fly's butt at three hundred yards—even farther—but the twenty-two ammunition was not accurate much past that.

Daniel slipped a box of twenty-two shells into his pocket and slipped the pistol into the shoulder holster he wore under his custom made jacket. He zipped the jacket halfway up and looked around again. Satisfied that he was still unseen, or at least unremarked, he replaced the false bottom and straightened the carpet that hid his goody box. "There," he said, "just a plain 'ol trunk."

He shut the trunk and put his foot up on the bumper. Clipped inside his boot was a double-edged knife. He checked to make sure it was in place then dropped his foot to the ground and shook his pant leg back down. In the pockets of his jacket, he had a bag of peanuts, a big bag of beef jerky—teriyaki, his favorite—several tissues and a few wet wipes, just in case. He walked around to the driver's door and retrieved a large bottle of water from inside.

One last time, he looked around. There was no one, anywhere. Of course, it didn't really matter because he wasn't doing anything wrong. He'd *never* actually done anything wrong, with the exception of the silenced pistol, and the pistol was a necessity; it was prudent to the business at hand.

Across the road a trailer park sat quietly in the gathering darkness, plain, nondescript, not unlike the thousands of others dotting the countryside. Unlike all those others, though, this one held Daniel's target. Skirting the tall wooden fence that surrounded the property, Daniel walked along, counting as he went. One, two... six... nine... eleven. Eleven roofs. Daniel peered over the fence at the numbers by the door. This was the correct address.

He waited. The minutes ticked by. One hour passed, then two. The sounds of dinner time and the laughter of children gave way to the murmuring sounds of many televisions. Brightly lit back yards dimmed one by one until he could only see a couple of lights from where he crouched. His target had still not arrived, but Daniel knew he would wait as long as he must.

"Danny Boy has the patience of old Job," his mother used to say.

They were all gone now, his mother, his father, his baby sis. They had once been living, vibrant people, giving love and receiving love. They had laughed, played, cried. And now they were dead.

And dead for what? The thrill of the kill? Dead because some piece of crap wanted a jolly? They were dead because of the human refuse Daniel was waiting for.

Daniel seldom considered his family now. Revenge was the reason he was here, but the intensity of it, the immediacy of his rage, had been lost in the time it had taken him to get here. The only emotions left to him were the cold-blooded calculations of a killer.

After his father's death, Daniel had taken the insurance money and invested it in himself. He took self-defense courses, shooting lessons, survival courses, and surveillance courses. He bought hardware, lots of hardware. Along with the obvious items, he purchased computers, tracking devices, and listening equipment, anything that seemed necessary or useful. Tonight he would get the return on his investment.

Sid Stearns. It was just a name and not uncommon. Daniel knew this because he had tracked down most of the Sid Stearns in the United States. But the Sid Stearns who lived in this trailer was the one, the *thing* that had taken everything and everyone Danny Boy loved. Sid Stearns was the catalyst that turned Danny into Daniel. Never again would he be Dan, Danny or Danny Boy. His innocence gone, Daniel was all about business.

As he waited, Daniel was not bored, as one might think. He was, in fact, excited, stimulated. He was thrilled, but a little sad. Soon his quest would be over. Before it was over, though, justice, true justice would be wrought. Tonight was the night.

As full darkness set in, Daniel saw lightening fork its way across the sky and felt a fine mist hit his face. Thunder boomed. "Great," he whispered. "It's going to be great."

***

"Great," Charlie muttered, "another friggin' storm."

He flipped on the Honda's wipers as sudden sheets of cold rain collided with the windshield. Charlie hated storms. He hated them bad. They scared him. The damp stink of them took him back to the nights he'd spent locked in the cellar by his drunk, abusive mother. She would leave him down there for days, sometimes. He would defecate and urinate in the empty fruit jars that lined the walls. Sometimes 'Mommy Dearest' would forget he was there and in desperation, he would have to drink his own urine. Oh, how he hated her.

But he'd repaid her—over and over. He'd lost count of the times he'd killed her. Of course, the first time she had died in the crash, the same crash that left Charlie with a limp. But she had come back. Charlie saw her, over and over, hiding in the eyes of *those women*. Charlie was wise to her, though, and he'd killed them all. A couple of times she had gender jumped, he guessed she was trying to fool him, and he had found her in a man. He killed them too. He would kill her as often as it took, wherever he found her and whoever she was. Charlie would not stop until she was really, truly dead.

The wipers swooshed back and forth across the windshield, then froze halfway. In seconds it was impossible for Charlie to see through the glass. He panicked and slammed his foot down hard on the brake. The old Honda fishtailed, then spun one hundred and eighty degrees, landing neatly in the ditch. Thankfully, there was no one else on the road.

Charlie was shaking as he opened the door. He was not hurt, and the car seemed to be okay, but the wheels were stuck deep in the mud. This storm had come up suddenly, but it had been raining all week, and the ground was soft. "Dammit," he muttered as he climbed the embankment to the road, "I'm so stupid! Stupid, stupid, stupid."

The fact of the matter was that Charlie *was* stupid, mostly. He was well below average intelligence, except when it came to finding Mother. Then he had the cunning of a fox. When not in that pursuit, though, he was just dumb old Charlie.

He paced up and down the side of the road, cursing and kicking at the puddles that formed in every depression. Soaked to the skin, he soon began to shiver from cold as well as fear. Finally, from way up ahead, he saw a light. Headlights! Salvation! As the car came closer, Charlie stuck out his thumb. The car began to slow. "Thank you, God!" he said, looking up at the darkened sky.

The vehicle was a big Lincoln, relatively new. It came to a stop, and the tinted power window on the driver's side slid halfway down. Charlie trotted across the pavement and looked in. The driver was a man, and there were no passengers.

"Hey, buddy, you all right?" the driver asked.

"Yeah, yeah. I just ran it off...wipers went out... you know." Charlie gestured toward the ditch and hoped the man would understand. "I'm wet and cold. I need a ride. I, ah—"

"You haven't been drinking or anything, have you? Because I don't want to be involved in helping someone evade the authorities. I believe in the law, yes sir! I don't cotton to drinking at all, and especially drinking and driving. My folks were killed by a drunk, and I had to grow up without 'em. I hate the bottle! I suppose that's why I took to preachin'."

The rain had plastered Charlie's hair to his head and was running off his shoulders in steady streams. He scrubbed a hand across his face and blinked a couple of times. "No, sir. I'm sober as a judge. I don't drink a drop! Well, of liquor. I do drink tea and coffee and pop, but no booze for me, no sir! I just slid off the pavement and…" Charlie furrowed his rain-soaked brow trying to think of something to say that would get the man to let him in the car. "You said you're a preacher? I go every Sunday, down to the Church of Christ. I clean the building on Saturdays, too!" Charlie was telling the truth. He was paid for it, but he did clean the church. He also attended most Sundays, unless he was on a mission to stop Mother.

"Well, you're one of God's own, so get in out of the rain."

The door locks popped. Charlie hurried around and got in on the passenger side. The man behind the wheel was big, probably six-four or six-five and he easily weighed two hundred and seventy-five pounds or more.

Charlie stuck out a wet hand. "Name's Charlie. Charlie Dunn. Thanks for stopping."

"Not a problem, Charlie Dunn. I'm Reverend Sidney Stearns."

As Charlie looked up into the man's eyes, he saw her. This man might call himself Sidney Stearns and be parading as a man of the cloth, but Charlie *knew*. Down inside there was 'Mommy Dearest.'" She had jumped again.

***

The Reverend pulled the big Lincoln back onto the road. "It's not fit to be out tonight, huh?"

"No, um, it's bad."

"What brings you out, Charlie?"

"Well, ah, I was, ah…looking for someone."

"Oh?"

"I was looking for my mother."

"Is she lost?"

"No, no. I believe I know where she is."

The Reverend drove on through the night. He wasn't *absolutely* sure, but he was mostly sure Charlie was a drunk—or at least a drinking man. Sidney hated drunks. He hated drinkers in general. It was a drunk who killed his mom and dad and left him an orphan. Because of a drunk, he was placed with his foster father who sodomized him repeatedly throughout the ten years

Sidney lived with him. His foster father had been a drinker too, a little. He was dead.

Now, Sid did 'The Lord's Work.' He knew he could not convert all the heathens, but he could smite the ungodly, so he searched out the intemperate and destroyed their flesh in order to save their eternal souls. He didn't worry over it much anymore. It was what he did.

"Where are you a preacher?" Charlie asked.

"Well, here and there. I'm not a pastor, Charlie, I am more like an evangelist. I make the path straight, purge out the wicked, drive out the devil."

"Oh," Charlie replied. "I thought you were...MY MOTHER!"

As he screamed the last words, Charlie drove a knife into the preacher's ribs. The car swerved, nearly out of control, but Sid held it tight. "YOU DEVIL!" he shouted, as he drove a wicked backhand into Charlie's face. The blow snapped Charlie's head backward and he slumped down in the seat.

Sid stomped on the brakes. The car skidded to a stop, and he slammed the shifter into park. He tore at his shirt in a frenzy. The Devil had stuck him! Was he going to die? He yanked open the glove box and fumbled out a flashlight, shining it on his wound.

With relief, he saw that the knife had caught on his suit jacket and had not penetrated more than an inch. Indeed, the blade was only three inches long, certainly not enough to kill him. The wound hurt, for sure, but the

Lord had been watching out for him. Sid pulled a white handkerchief from his pocket, rolled it up and tucked it against the wound. The bleeding would stop. He thought, briefly, about a doctor, but that might lead to questions he didn't want to answer.

After resting a moment, Sid checked Charlie for a pulse. "So, you are alive, huh Devil? Well, we will fix that. I will drive you from this vessel. Yes, I will destroy the vessel, but…"

Sid got out of the car and went back to the trunk, where he retrieved rope and duct tape. Ten minutes later he placed a bound and gagged Charlie into the trunk, turned the car around and headed for home.

"There is much work to do tonight," he muttered happily to himself, "much work!" In his anticipation, he almost forgot about the wound in his side. After a few moments he could hear Charlie stirring in the trunk. "Good," he whispered, and smiled. He preferred them to struggle.

Sid drove on through the night humming 'Onward Christian Soldiers.' He would have company tonight.

What Sid didn't know, though, was that he already had a guest.

***

"Dammit to hell!" Daniel spat, and kicked impatiently at the ground with the toe of his shoe. He had not brought rain gear, an amateur mistake, and he was soaked to his skin. He thought to retreat to the car—the heater in the Chevy worked well, and he longed to be warm. He actually took a couple of steps toward the car before he could stop himself.

"Stupid, stupid, stupid." He clapped his hand over his mouth. He was losing it, talking out loud to himself. He'd spent so much time learning, preparing. Now, in the moment of truth, he couldn't make the grade. Maybe he should abort the mission, come back later. He stiffened himself and shook his head slightly. No, tonight had to be the night.

But he was still wet.

He peered through the slats in the fence and an idea occurred to him. A few splinters later he stood on the porch and eyed the lock on the door. His training had included a couple of locksmith courses, and in less than thirty seconds he was inside.

Closing the door behind him, Daniel looked around in surprise. A single bulb burning in the kitchen cast enough light for him to see the place was amazingly clean. Daniel had not expected his family's killer to be neat. In Daniel's imagination, Sid Stearns was a sub-human creature living in filth and debris. Scattered beer cans, dirty rags, and rotting trash were what he'd envisioned, not this quaint, orderly scene before him.

The furniture in the room was not expensive, but it was clean, well matched, and arranged to give the place a cozy feel. In the wall directly opposite the door, a heavy wooden mantle lined with photographs in decorative frames topped a gas fireplace. In front of the couch was a large oak coffee table. The only item on the table was a large Bible. For a moment Daniel believed he had made a mistake, broken into the wrong house.

"Damn. This is *not* going as planned." He crossed the room to the mantle, leaving a wet trail, and squinted at the pictures. His target appeared in at least three of them.

His target: Sidney Robert Stearns. Height: six foot, four inches. Weight: 285 pounds. Eyes: blue. Hair: brown. Distinguishing marks: a scar on the left shoulder, no tattoos. Family history: unknown. Occupation: unknown.

The litany ran through Daniel's mind as he stared at the pictures. He didn't care who the other people in the photos were, only the target mattered. He turned from the mantle and looked around the room, searching for the best place to wait. Light flashed through the window blinds, and the decision was made for him as a car pulled into the space in front of the trailer.

Daniel panicked. This was not going the way he had planned. He was a novice, a blooming idiot! Bolting through the first door he saw, he found himself sprawled across a queen-sized bed. His momentum carried him over the far edge, and he tore off the bedspread as he fell to the floor. His flailing arm hit the bedside table, sending the items atop it crashing against the wall.

"Shit," he whispered after everything had settled back to silence. Then he heard footsteps on the gravel outside. He was caught.

He forced down his panic and shuffled cautiously toward the bedroom door, trying not to kick any of the items that now littered the floor. He eased the twenty-two from its holster and flipped the safety off. He placed his finger on the hair-trigger as he neared the doorframe. A thud next to him surprised him, and he looked over to see feathers floating down in the gloom. He'd fired the gun accidentally.

At this point, Daniel considered leaping through the bedroom window. He just wanted to be gone. He should have waited outside, thought things out a little better. Footsteps thumped on the porch, and the front door opened. He set his jaw. It was now or never.

Daniel burst through the bedroom door into the front room. He saw a man, a target, come through the door. Daniel pulled the trigger, over and over. He hit the man, saw him jerk with each round, but something was dreadfully wrong. The target appeared to be wrapped in plastic, bound with duct tape and rope. The dull thud of the .22 slugs striking flesh and bone echoed in his ears. Patches of blood bloomed, almost magically, behind the macabre Saran wrap.

This was wrong. This was not his target. More than anything in the world Daniel wanted to stop, but his finger continued to work the trigger. How many rounds had he fired? He'd forgotten to count. He was nothing but a rank amateur—worse, a kid with a gun, a petrified punk.

Finally, Daniel regained control of his finger. The plastic wrap man lurched forward a step or two and fell to the floor. He had at least a dozen holes in him and, to Daniel's credit, they were all dead center mass. The problem lay in the fact that he had just pumped twelve rounds into Charles Dunn.

Daniel stared at the man on the floor. Where was Sid Stearns? Desperately, he tried to remember how many shots he had fired. The pistol held fourteen. One in the bedroom, then one, two, three... Events had taken on a surreal quality for Daniel, and he was unable to focus. Sid Stearns stepped around the doorframe and reached for him. Daniel tried to raise the gun to fire, but it was no use. As he jerked his hand up, he fired his last bullet harmlessly into the floor. The slide jammed open, the weapon was empty.

Daniel clawed for his boot knife, but it was way too late. He could see, but not stop, the giant fist coming at his face. The blow was bone-shattering but amazingly painless. Everything just went black.

***

Daniel awoke bound and gagged. He was not in Stearns trailer house. This was another place, perhaps a warehouse or a barn. He could smell used oil and grease, and something musty, like rotting straw. Why wasn't he dead? Surely he must be in for some heinous type of torture.

His head throbbed. He longed to feel his injury, to poke gingerly at the bruised flesh, as is instinctual in all of us, but his weak struggles left him riding waves of nausea. He closed his eyes and concentrated on taking shallow, even breaths. After a moment his stomach settled and he could think clearly again.

What had happened? He remembered the shooting. He had killed someone, but not Stearns. Who, then? And where was Stearns?

Daniel didn't have long to wonder. Not half an hour after he regained consciousness, he heard an engine approach and the light crunch of wheels rolling across hard packed dirt. A car door slammed, and terror washed over Daniel, just as it had in the trailer house. He broke out in a sweat. Seconds ticked by like hours. A lock rattled. Daniel's eyes rolled toward the sound just as the door slid open. Silhouetted in the doorway was a huge black figure, but that was all Daniel could see through the blinding morning sunlight. The door slid closed, but Daniel's vision was impaired by the large black blot burned on his retina. As the image faded, Daniel could see Stearns. He was carrying a jug and a plastic bag, and he was walking toward Daniel.

Because of the sudden blinding light, Daniel was unable to make out color clearly, but his imagination supplied the red color needed to make the jug a gas can. No imagination was required to believe Stearns was capable of burning him alive. Daniel's heart pounded as Stearns walked over and peered down at him.

"Well, you are awake! Glad to see you're okay. I was afraid I'd given you too much sedative. But you're a strong young lad, aren't you?" Stearns bent forward and ripped the tape off Daniel's mouth, then turned away and placed the jug and the bag on a nearby table.

Daniel's face burned, but he tried not to show his pain and fear. "Now what happens?"

Stearns looked over and said, "that's up to you."

"Up to me?"

From the bag, Stearns removed several food items and some paper cups. He poured liquid from the jug into one of the cups and Daniel realized it was orange juice, not gasoline. What did Stearns have up his sleeve?

"Look, kid, if I wanted you dead, you'd be dead." After the blunders he had made, Daniel knew that was the plain truth. "I will untie one of your hands so you can eat. You've been out for almost two days. You're dehydrated."

"*Two days?*"

"I had to clean up." Stearns shook his head and sat down in a creaky wooden chair. "I'm pulling out. I've had two close calls now, and well…I guess I got a little sloppy, a little proud. I used to be so careful, but now, well, I just need some time."

Daniel looked at Stearns with genuine amazement. This was the man who had killed his family?

Stearns realized Daniel was staring at him. "What?"

"Nothing…It's just—"

"Just what?"

"Why didn't you kill me? Are you going to torture me? Rape me? What?"

Stearns sprayed the orange juice he had just sipped all over his lap. "My goodness, boy! *Rape* you? What the hell do you think I am? I am a man of *God!* I *purge* evil from this world!"

"You killed my mother, my father and my little baby sister, you son of a bitch!"

"Oh, is that what this is about?" Stearns relaxed back in his chair. "You say I killed your mother, father, and sister? When?"

"Three years ago. Paducah, Kentucky."

Stearns thought for a long moment. "Oh, yes, I remember now."

"How in the hell do you forget something like that?"

"Well, uh, I am a busy man, and I've had a lot of encounters with...evil."

"*Evil*? My little sister was ten years old!"

"And for that, I am truly sorry. She...It was an accident. I didn't mean to kill her. She stepped into the path of the bullet. She...she died in my arms."

Stearns' voice cracked at the end, and he dropped his face into his hands. Daniel lay silent for a full minute then asked in a flat voice, "what about my mother and father?"

Stearns looked up, surprised. "They were drunks! I saw them at that restaurant many times. They were *always* drinking. They got what they deserved." Stearns leaned toward Daniel with an intense look. "A drunk killed my parents leaving me to be raised by a filthy child molester." After a moment his shoulders drooped, and the heat went out of his gaze. "I am sorry about the child, though. Didn't you ever make a mistake?"

Daniel thought about the man he had killed. "Ah…"

Stearns poured Daniel a glass of juice and helped him rise to a sitting position. "Drink this. You've been out 'nigh on to thirty-six hours." Daniel finished the glass but waved it away when Stearns offered more. Stearns chuckled at him. "Boy, you have a lot to learn. And you have taught me a thing or two; I looked over your car! You have some fancy gadgets, and I bet you have a lot of technical knowledge, but in this game hands-on is what you need." With that, Stearns turned and walked to the door.

"What now?" Daniel asked.

"You're on your own. Look, you killed an innocent man—at least *you* think he's innocent, and so will the cops. You stalked me and broke into my home. What are you going to do? Call the cops? By the time you get loose, I will be long gone. Stearns pulled a knife from his pocket and dropped it to the ground at his feet. "We're done—for now, anyway. Your car is parked outside, and the keys are in the ignition. When you get loose, eat something. There are cold cuts and sweets there on the table. Goodbye."

Stearns turned and walked out the door. Daniel, wisely, looked away until the door closed.

Once he heard the car drive away, Daniel worked his way over to the knife. The ropes were not hard to cut, and he thought, for just a moment, to give chase. Stearns was right, though, Daniel was guilty of murder. He, like Stearns, had killed an innocent while trying to take out a target. Besides, he was too weak to try.

Breakfast beckoned him from the table, so he poured a glass of juice, picked up a doughnut and sat down on a bale of straw. After a few doughnuts, he lay back and fell asleep.

It was dark when he woke, but he felt stronger. He sat up and stretched, splaying his fingers out as far as they would go. When he did, something hit the floor in front of him. It was Stearns' knife. He gazed at it for a moment, in the deepening gloom, and wondered what it would tell him if it could talk. Hefting it by the blade, he raised his arm, as though to throw it away, then, on a whim, tucked it in his pocket instead.

True to his word, Stearns had left Daniel's keys in the ignition. Daniel got in and drove away. He never looked back.

***

Three months had passed since The Incident, as Daniel thought of it. Three long months. He often thought of Stearns, and of the unknown man—Mr. Nobody, the first man he had killed. Stearns, above all others, was responsible for molding Daniel into the cold killing machine he had become.

Daniel had twelve kills now, all up close and personal. As he watched his target move about her house, he fingered the knife—Stearns knife. Tonight, once again, it would do its job. Another target, another kill. Someday, perhaps, he would find Stearns. Or not.

It was enough for Daniel that he had made the switch. With each sanction, the frightened and insecure Daniel ebbed away. His pain eased, Daniel was now the hunter, not the victim. He would repay society for what it had done to Stearns and, ultimately, to himself.

After all, what comes around, goes around…and around…

The End

Special thanks to Aphelion Ezine for first publication of this story in 2007.

DEATH

When I awoke, the room was unnaturally cold. Shivering, I drew my covers closer and rolled over to look at the illuminated numbers on the clock: 6:66. I sighed and said into the dark, "Very funny. Don't you have something else to do?"

"Good morning, Winston." His voice was soothing—masculine, but soft and unaccented.

As my eyes adjusted, I began to appreciate just how dark the room was. Dawn was still an hour away, and the only light came from the red numbers on the clock. It was always that way when he came, cold and dark.

I could smell coffee. It was obvious he wanted to talk. I yawned, then sat up and clicked on the lamp. In a wing back chair near the bed sat a dark figure. A sweet aroma surrounded him, musky, almost comforting, but even though the chair was lit by the lamp, his face was shrouded in darkness. In each hand, he held a large steaming cup. "Here," he offered, holding out one of the cups.

I pushed my pillows against the headboard and propped myself up, then took the cup from his hand and sipped the steaming liquid. *He may be Death*, I thought, *but he makes a* hell *of a latte.*

***

He was dressed, as he always was, in a suit. There was no long hooded robe, no sickle, he looked more like a banker than the Grim Reaper.

"This is good," I said. "Where did you get it?"

"Paris," he answered. "There is a great little café near the tower. And their croissants! Ah, to die for!" He chuckled. "You know the place, I believe."

"Perhaps," I grumbled. "I, ah…I did some work in Paris, back in the late eighties. I didn't really care for it. I'm not a big fan of French cuisine."

"You want breakfast?"

"Uh, no thank you. I—"

"Want to know why I'm here?"

I looked at him over the rim of my cup. Except for the unnerving way his face was always shadowed, he could have been anyone. He was nondescript, some would even consider him handsome in a mild sort of way. He had light colored hair, blue eyes, and a thick brown mustache. He could have been the guy next door, your cab driver, the cop in the cruiser, your doctor, or your own brother. I found myself looking away quickly.

My eyes fell on the .45 caliber pistol that lay on the bedside table. It was a good weapon. I'd had it since my military days. It had been modified, somewhat, and fitted with a silencer.

"Why do you keep it?" he asked, following my gaze. "You know you're not slated to go for a long, long time."

"So *you* say."

His lips thinned. "I'm Death, not the liar."

"I just feel better keeping it near." I smiled. "It may not be my time to die, but there are a hell of a lot of bad things that can happen to a fellow besides dying."

He almost chuckled. "I suppose."

"So what brings you by at this ungodly hour? I mean, when the death angel awakens you—"

"Angel? In all these years you've never referred to me as an angel. I *was* an angel..." He trailed off with a distant look.

"Hey, don't get so serious."

He closed his eyes and straightened his tie. "Yes, of course."

I watched him sip his drink. After a moment I set mine on the bedside table. "You okay?"

"I'm not here for me. I don't need your, ah, services."

"So tell me, you haven't always been Mr. Death, the Soul Snatcher, the Big Dirt Napster?"

He sniffed. "Heavens, no. I have not always been in my present state of—how should I say it? Servitude? Yes, that's it. I haven't always *served* the way I do now."

"So how did you get the job?"

"I was talked into it. I mean, well, that confounded Satan! You know him."

"Well, I, ah…really don't."

He chuckled. "You know what I mean. Anyway, it was only supposed to be temporary. It seemed like a good idea at the time. I mean, for goodness sakes, there were only *two* people on the planet. What are there now, six billion? I really thought we would reconcile."

I could see he was uncomfortable talking about it. I almost laughed at the thought of *me* making the Grim Reaper uncomfortable. I should have changed the subject, but I'm inquisitive by nature. "You know, I've always wondered how you do it."

"Do what?"

"Well, people die every second, several a second. Even at light speed—"

"It doesn't work that way, Winston. I have a lot of help. Actually, I just oversee it all. I am rarely on hand for any singular event, just a few of the more interesting ones. Which brings me to the point. I need your help."

"I figured as much."

The first time I met him, I thought I must be insane, but after watching him interact with other people, I realized that, while *I* might be delusional, they all were not. Death even had me hire a photographer to take his picture—he turned out to be quite photogenic.

For a while I thought he must be an agent sent to lead me on some diabolical mission—some hold-over from my old life—but he performed several stunts that no human could have managed. Now I have no doubt he is who he claims to be. He is Death, the Grim Reaper himself.

He is also my employer, in a manner of speaking.

"You know I helped you a lot before I started this latest gig," I said.

"You did, in fact, kill a lot of people, but that did not help me, nor any of my minions." He leaned forward and winked at me. "You may not realize this, Winston, but at the present time you have the highest number of individual events of any person alive."

"You're trying to tell me I've killed more people than anyone ever has?"

"I did not say that. What I said was that of all the people now alive, you have personally committed the highest number of individual acts. There are those who have killed a lot more people than you, but they were mostly group efforts using mechanical means."

"Hey," I smiled uneasily, "I was good, what can I say? But I'm retired, remember?" I found no humor, no pleasure, in what I had been.

"I'm sorry, Winston," the Reaper said, sounding genuine. "I was not trying to assign any moral judgment to your past activities, I was only trying to explain why I need you. Aside from being one of the most proficient killers on the planet, no offense, you are also one of the only people that I converse with who does not fear me. As a matter of fact, in all the times I've been near you, I've *never* sensed fear in you. Even that time you believed you were dying, you still—"

"But you said my time..."

He looked puzzled for a moment, then, "Oh! I was not there for you, silly boy. There were several other dead folks around, remember?"

"I, uh...yeah." My voice dropped to a hoarse whisper. "Well, fear... You have to *care* to fear."

Death shook his head. "Enough of this somber talk. Look I know how you hate to be bothered so early in your day, but I need your help on one."

"Just one? I started out with one a long time ago." I yawned, covering my mouth with the back of my hand. "Tell me why I do this again?"

"Penance?" Death offered, coming as close to laughing as he ever did.

"Can it wait a couple of hours?"

"Well, truthfully this s.o.b. is driving me nuts. I am at my wits' end here."

"You're Death, for pete's sake. Can't you just tell him to shut the hell up?"

"I wish," he grumbled. "Look, this guy, well he was very high up in the United States government a few years back, and now, as you can guess, he's a little upset about his passing. He is threatening to haunt the hell out of the White House and reveal all kinds of secrets to Russia, China and so on. He will start a damn nuclear war or worse if he can get anyone to listen, and believe me when I tell you, there *are* people who will listen—especially that damn Kim Jong-un in Korea! I'll be glad when that bastard's day comes. I am going to get him *personally*."

"Whoa, whoa!" I said, trying to sound calm. After all, if Death was worried, it must be time for me to be worried. "You know, I've been helping—uh—working for you for what, seven and a half, eight years, now? I've *never* heard you curse. This *must* be serious. How much trouble can this guy cause? Who is—was—he anyway?"

"You didn't see the news late last night, I take it."

"No. I was out." He handed me the morning paper. The headline was big and bold. "Man! I can't believe he's gone! Damn, he wasn't even that old. What got him anyway?"

Death tapped his chest. "Ticker."

"I thought he got all that straightened out." I glanced over the story. "He appears to have died in his sleep."

"All the worse," Death groaned. "He doesn't believe he's really dead."

"And you can't stop him from haunting?"

"No."

"Have you explained the consequences?"

"Of course I have, but he's a damnable politician! Look, Winston, can you talk to him?"

"Yeah, sure," I said. "Besides, I actually met him a couple of times. He was my boss several years ago."

"That's another matter. I sort of...well, I told him about our arrangement."

"What did he say?"

"He claimed he ordered your assassination several years back and believes you're dead. He thinks this is part of some elaborate plot."

"I see. Do you think this is a good idea? I mean, don't you have some other poor soul that does this same sort of work?"

"No, you're it. Well, okay, you're the only one who speaks English."

"What? Doesn't he speak Russian, French, *something?*"

"Ha, ha, ha," Death said in a monotone.

"Oh, all right. Let me get showered and I'll see him in my office in one hour." I looked at Death with a cold smile. "Besides, I want to see the prick who ordered my *unsuccessful* assassination."

"Thanks," Death said, "I owe you one."

With that he was gone, leaving the room noticeably brighter. I sipped my latte and read the rest of the news article, then crawled out of bed, chuckling. "He should have laid off the quarter-pounders."

I showered, dressed and went downstairs. For obvious reasons my office was in my home and my clients *always* came to me. I dimmed the lights before I sat down at the desk. Drawing a deep breath, I ran my hand over the big blue crystal ball on my desk. The crystal turned to crimson, and I waited.

After a moment an eerie black hole appeared in the wall facing me. It started out no bigger than a pinprick and spiraled out to about seven feet in diameter when it was fully open. It unnerved me every time I saw it. I could, it seemed, hear muted screams accompanied by the faintest whiff of sulfur. The most upsetting part, however, was the unearthly cold that issued from the hole in foggy tendrils that twisted around the furniture legs and up under the cuffs of my pants.

Presently I could see three figures materializing inside the blackness. I had seen the two escorts before— at least I think they were the same two. They were big, black, hulking figures whose faces were hidden beneath their hoods. I suspected I should be thankful for that. Their robes were rags, layer upon layer of coarse black cloth, and the thickness of their garments added to their considerable bulk. I suspected the robes had been nice, once, but years, millennia, of wear and tear... I recognized the third figure as well, though it had been several years.

The portal now stretched from floor to ceiling and was twice as wide, but as the three stepped through into my office, it snapped shut instantly. It opened slow but closed in the blink of an eye.

My patient was visibly angry. It was quite obvious he was unaccustomed to being manhandled. An overstuffed leather chair sat opposite me, about three feet beyond my desk. The big black demons slammed their detainee into the seat and disappeared.

The patient turned his head quickly to either side. "Where did they go?"

"They're still here."

"To hell, you say! Who are you? I'll tell you what, you sons of bitches are in a lot of trouble! Just wait. I still have connections. You don't just kidnap somebody like me!"

I could hear the southern twang in his voice, not much different than my own—we had, after all, been born and raised in the same state.

"There's going to be hell to pay! You listening to me, boy?" He tried to stand but was slammed back into the chair by a pair of unseen hands.

"I told you they were still there."

"What? Where?" He tried to stand again, with the same outcome. He tensed for a moment and drew a deep breath, then sagged as though someone had let all the air out of him. "What do you people want?" he whined. "I...I can't help you. I don't know much anymore. I do have money. What do you want? I..." He hunched over in the chair and covered his face with his hands. For a moment he seemed broken, but when he looked up, there was a flicker of defiance in his eyes. "I demand to know right now what you want."

I leaned forward and folded my hands together on the desk. "What I want, sir, is to help you. Whether you believe me or not, is up to you." I smiled. "I *am* a doctor. I hold a Ph.D. in psychology and psychiatry."

"Your name!" He hammered his fist on the arm of his chair. "What is your name?"

"Winston," I said. "Winston MacQue."

The look on his face was priceless. "But you are dead! I know! I ordered…"

"No, Mr. President, the attempt was unsuccessful. However, sir, I have something to tell you." He looked at me expectantly but did not respond. "*You*, sir, *are* dead. Graveyard, cemetery, doornail, *dead.*

He looked around the study nervously. "I…uh—"

"Sit back, sir," I said in a casual tone. "Let's look at this for a moment and try to sort."

He settled back into the leather seat with all the ease of a man on the wrong end of a gun. I sighed. It was going to be a long day.

We talked through the morning and into the early afternoon. At first he was somewhat reluctant to speak to me but, as time wore on, he loosened up. "Look," I said finally, "I need to go to the bathroom, and I'd like to grab a bite to eat. You no longer need to do these things, but I am still tied to this mortal body."

He creased his brow. "Come to think of it, I haven't eaten since last night. That's not like me."

"If you have any ideas about leaving, don't. They will prevent you from doing so." When I left the room, he was staring at the floor. I felt kind of sorry for the old boy, even if he had ordered my death.

I came back thirty minutes later, and he was still in the same position he'd been in when I left. I walked over and leaned against the front of my desk. I held a cup of coffee in my hand. "I would have brought you one, but I knew you wouldn't want it."

"Uh, yeah."

I waved the coffee under his nose. "Smell it."

"It…ah, I can't smell it. It doesn't *have* any smell."

"Yes, it does. You just can't smell it. It's steaming, right?"

"Yes."

"So it would stand to reason it is hot. Try it. There will be no taste and no warmth."

He sipped at it, frowned, and then took a big drink. When he handed it back, half was gone.

"No taste, no heat, right?" He nodded glumly. "That's the way it is, sir. You will not have those senses for awhile—maybe never again."

His shoulders sagged, and he looked like a weary hound dog. "Never again?"

"Look, right now you are in a kind of limbo. You have a couple of options. You can go *on*, or you can go haunt, which is what I was told you wish to do."

"Who told you that?"

"Death."

142

"Oh."

I tried to smile. "Look, I was in the spy game for several years, and I participated in more than a few sanctions. I know the kinds of things that go on, but I must tell you if you choose to go haunting the effects could be devastating—not only to your soul, but to the world as well. If you follow through with your threats then, well, you could be damning yourself to a fate worse than death—no pun intended." I walked around the desk and sat down in my chair. I placed my elbows on the desk, folded my hands together and leaned forward intently. "I don't claim to know the state of your soul, but I've *never* been visited by someone who is at peace."

He broke down. "Dear God, I am so sorry. Why, oh God, why? Why did I do it all? Winston, I am sorry. Can you help me?" He looked at me desperately. Tears were streaming down his face.

"I watched him calmly, waiting for his fit to subside. "Sir, it's not up to me. Until now my job has been to convince the dead they *are dead.* You are the first one Death has ever asked me to try and talk out of haunting."

"Well, I just don't know *what* to do."

"Sir, you have the right to haunt. I just would not recommend it, that's all." I regarded him across the desk for a moment. "I would like to know one thing, however. What is it that you know that's got Death so worried? Could you really cause that much trouble?"

He motioned for me to come closer. I leaned forward, but he waved me closer. I sighed, got up and walked around the desk again. I leaned over him, and he whispered in my ear. My jaw dropped. By the time he finished speaking my head was spinning, and I had to lean against the desk to keep from falling over. I had heard and seen a lot in my day, but even *I* wasn't ready for *this*. I returned to my seat, sat back and closed my eyes.

"So," I finally said, "what are you going to do?"

He shook his head sadly. "I just don't know."

In the next instant, a cold gust blew through the room, scattering papers and knocking pictures from the walls. The crystal on my desk flashed crimson again, and the room went all but black.

"YOU TOLD HIM!"

He cringed in his chair. "I—I'm sorry! I didn't mean to! I—"

"TAKE HIM! And may God damn him to everlasting darkness!"

Light returned to the room. Death stood before me, dressed as usual and shaking with fury. He drew a deep breath and visibly calmed himself. In a low, measured tone he said, "Winston, I have never said this before. I am sorry, and I am scared."

With that, he was gone, and I was left alone to contemplate the most awful thing that had ever been revealed to me. I picked up the phone. I didn't want to be alone—not ever again.

***

I awoke the next morning in the arms of a beautiful woman. Zoe and I had been seeing each other for several weeks, and I believed I loved her, though it was hard for me to tell. After Death began to visit me, I was unsure of much. Zoe was a devout Catholic, which made her willingness to spend the night with me all the more amazing.

I could smell coffee. I slid from the bed without waking her and went to the kitchen. *He* was there.

"Winston, you're awake! I took the liberty."

"Thanks."

Death poured a cup and handed it to me. "About yesterday, I am sorry you had to find out like that. I mean, what a rotten way to learn of it."

"What difference does it make?" I said, staring out the window. There were children across the street, a boy and a girl, obviously brother and sister. The boy was teaching the girl to ride a bike. I had always wanted kids.

I turned and looked at Death, just looked at him. His face seemed kind and good, his eyes sad. It was probably an illusion.

"Nothing can be done?" I asked.

"Not now."

"So if nothing can be done, what difference would it make if the ex-prez went public?"

"It's not yet time."

I slammed my mug down on the counter, sloshing hot coffee over the rim and burning my hand. I didn't flinch. "You want this, don't you?"

"No, Winston, I do not. Look, son," he said, touching my hand soothingly, "I didn't do any of this. I was duped, just like you."

"I'd like to believe you."

"What do you believe?"

"I…I don't know. One question—how many people are infected?"

"Everyone."

"Don't kid me, I am a doctor, you know. Any time you introduce a virus, a poison, anything like that, there is always a percentage of organisms in any given population that have natural immunity. It's a known medical fact."

He shook his head. "Not this time, son. It was genetically designed. Everyone is infected."

"So how long?"

"Months, a year, maybe two. No more than that."

"Is there a vaccine?"

"Sure," he replied, "it's here now. You can get it if you know what to ask for, but there's a price."

"A price?"

"The Mark."

"The mark?"

"Revelations," he explained, "the Mark of the Beast."

"You've got to be kidding! I don't believe—"

"You don't believe what? You don't believe everything you've seen? Everything you've experienced?"

I stared out the window for several long minutes. What could I say? What could I do? Nothing.

"So what did the old prez decide to do?"

"Oh, he went on."

"To what?"

"Don't know. It's not up to me. I just collect 'em and pass 'em on. I couldn't tell you what happens after that. You know, you've saved a lot of lives."

"How's that? So now, instead of getting toasted by nukes, they can die long and agonizing deaths from a hemorrhagic virus?"

"Now they will have a choice. You gave them that choice."

"I feel really great about that."

"Look, Win—" he began.

"Win. My dad used to call me Win."

A strange look crossed his face. "I mean Winston," he corrected. "Nothing is quite as it seems. Nothing. What do you *really* believe?"

"I just don't know."

"Well, it's up to you. I have to go."

"Will I see you again?"

"Probably."

He got up from the table and walked out the front door. He had never done that before. I watched through the window as he walked down the sidewalk. A long black limo pulled alongside the curb. The driver got out and opened the rear door. Death started to step in, then paused, watching the kids for a moment. He turned and waved to me. Instinctively, I waved back. He got in, and the driver closed the door. As they pulled away, a voice spoke up behind me.

"Winston, did you know your front door is open?" Zoe stood by the kitchen door wearing one of my shirts and nothing else.

"Oh, yeah. An old...friend...came by for coffee."

"You should have introduced us! I mean, I don't know any of your friends."

I smiled sadly. "You will meet him soon enough, Zoe." I pulled her against me and began to weep.

"Winston, what's wrong?"

"Zoe, do you love me?"

She leaned back and looked up at my face. "Well, yes. Yes, I do."

"Will you marry me?"

"Are you sure?"

"Yes. I have never been more sure of anything."

"Then, yes! Yes, I will. Now, may I have a cup of that coffee? It smells wonderful."

I poured it for her, and she sipped it.

"Mmm. Winston, this is the best coffee I've ever tasted!"

"He may be Death," I muttered, "but he makes a hell of a cup of coffee."

"What was that, dear?"

"Nothing, honey. Nothing."

***

Zoe and I were married. She insisted on being married by her priest, who would not marry us unless I converted to Catholicism, so I did.

I lay awake on our wedding night, thinking of our vows. Love, honor, cherish, deliver us from evil. Zoe had put that last in. I thought about the .45 in the drawer. I planned to use it first on Zoe and then on myself. It was the only way to save us from the horrors ahead. I knew I had to do it, but not tonight. Maybe tomorrow. I drifted off to sleep with her in my arms and 'deliver us from evil' echoing in my head. I had never wanted anything more.

I woke the next morning with a new plan. I still knew a few people, had a few contacts. If I could get enough proof, I could go to the media. If enough people were willing to fight, we could force those with the cure to make enough for everyone. We could thwart the Devil's plan! I was quite fired up.

But after two weeks of dragging a bewildered Zoe in and out of offices in Washington D.C., I was no longer quite so sure of myself. Unable to come right out and ask, lest I give myself away too soon, I was forced to hint, to intimate, to suggest. Most of my conversations ended with the suggestion that I seek professional help.

Finally, armed with nothing more than a few enigmatic comments made by a senator's aide, I went to a television station. I wanted to talk to someone, to share this burden with anyone who might be able to help. Zoe and I sat in the car across the street from the station as I finally told her what was going on and, bless her, she believed every word without question. Tears filled her eyes, but determination steeled her voice. She would not give up as long as we both lived.

The next thing I saw was a red dot on her forehead. Before I could move, the dot expanded to a black hole. Her eyes widened in surprise, then she slumped down in the seat. I had just enough time to scream, "NO!" before searing heat filled my brain and blackness overtook me.

**

I woke to a bright new day and a lot of unusual commotion. I thought I could hear children. Zoe bustled in with a laundry basket tucked under her arm. "You better get downstairs, your dad is here."

"My dad? My dad has been dead for—"

"Dead?" Zoe laughed. "He's not dead as far as I can tell, and he's got those kids all stirred up. You'd better get in there and settle things down."

"Kids?"

"Yeah, kids. You know, our children? Two boys, one girl." Worry creased her forehead. "Win, are you okay?"

"Ah…yeah, sure."

I dressed and went down to the front room. Death sat on the couch playing with three kids who apparently belonged to me. He still looked the same, but today he wore a white suit.

He looked up and smiled as I entered the room. "Hey, how are you?"

"A little confused."

"Don't worry about it," he chuckled.

Zoe called the children and herded them into the kitchen for breakfast.

I sat down on the couch. "So what is all this?"

"What is the last thing you remember?"

"Dying."

"Well, what did you think the hereafter would be like, anyway?"

"Uh…I don't know. Do you mean I'm dead?"

"In a manner of speaking."

"No kidding! I thought I'd surely go to hell. I mean, I killed—"

"Forgiven."

"Because of what I did with the prez?"

"No, son, because of your faith. You can't *work* your way here. So look, a couple of things. First, they," he pointed into the other room, "don't know about the old world, and this world has two moons. Oh, and I'm your dad. I live next door."

"Dad?"

"Yeah, well, I was getting tired of the old gig."

Zoe poked her head through the door. "Hey, do you guys want breakfast?"

Death stood up quickly. "I'll make the coffee."

I sat on the couch listening to the happy voices in the kitchen. Could this be real? After a bit Death came back with two cups of coffee. I sipped it. It was good. "You know, Dad, you make a hell of a cup of coffee."

"*Heck*," he said sternly. "Watch the language, son."

I couldn't help but grin.

The End

NEVER ASK WHY

"Here kitty, kitty, kitty. Here kitty, kitty, kitty, kitty. Come here, Yoda." Roger picked up the big Norwegian Forest cat. "Hey, Yoda," he said as he stroked the big cat's back, "I need your help, boy. Come on, you are going to take a trip. Not far." Inside his gut, Roger felt a tightness. He'd raised Yoda from a kitten. He thought back on the day that Yoda had come to live with him. He was going into Walmart, and some lady out front was giving away kittens. She had one left when Roger peered into the box.

"He's yours, Mister," the older, overweight woman wheezed.

"I…ah…I can't." Roger said, as he smiled politely. "I don't have the time."

"Well," she said, under labored breaths, "if somebody doesn't take him, he's goin' to the pound to be gassed. I gotta get home and get on my oxygen. I got the emphysema, you know. This heat…" the woman wheezed again. Roger smiled politely again and walked into the store. He had concluded his shopping and was leaving when he saw the heavyset cat woman walking toward the parking lot.

"Get rid of him?" Roger asked.

"Hell, no," the woman said, "but I got to go, I can't breathe." Roger looked into the box. The kitten was cute and, quite frankly, Roger had both the room and the time for a cat. What Roger also had were mice, lots of mice. A cat would be a good thing, one would think, but Roger did not want his mice killed. They were what are commonly referred to as lab rats, but they were actually Canadian white mice. Roger had about a hundred of them, and he used them in many experiments in his lab. He did not want a cat terminating months of his work prematurely just because the feline was following its natural instincts. Roger's lab was in his home. It *was* his home, but, throwing caution to the wind, he had taken the kitten. He'd named it 'Yoda.' Yoda, to date, had not killed a single mouse.

"Well, except that one time," Roger said out loud as he stroked the cat. "Yes, you did." He smiled. "You killed the one that got out." Roger opened the door of a strange looking device. It looked very similar to an old-style phone booth, except it was airtight and there was a massive transformer sitting on top of it. Yoda protested somewhat and began to pace along the floor of the apparatus. Roger moved to a long control panel. He flipped switches and made notes of readings on gauges and meters. He turned on audio and video equipment, his hands were a blur of activity. Finally, one last switch was all he needed to throw. "Yoda," Roger spoke softly to the booth, "you'll make it. You're not a mouse, and you won't run off like that damn dog. You'll be okay. I— uh—I promise." Roger's hands trembled a bit. He took a deep breath and then quickly flicked the switch. The booth lit up, and Yoda disappeared.

Roger held his breath. A few feet from the booth sat a wooden platform covered with carpeting. Roger watched the platform. It was three feet high and four feet by four feet on top. It was just a simple wooden box Roger had cobbled together, however, it served a purpose.

"Ten. Nine. Eight. Seven." Roger counted under his breath. "Three. Two. One. Zero." No Yoda. Roger's stomach sank. "Yoda," he whispered, "I'm sorry, boy."

Roger's eyes dropped to the console. Suddenly a flash of light appeared above the platform.

"Me…ow…ow." The cat appeared, giving Roger a start. The feline leaped from the platform, landing on the lab floor. Roger approached his pet, and the big Norwegian Forest cat hissed, showing his formidable teeth.

"Easy, boy," Roger spoke softly, trying to calm the beast. "Come on, kitty," he continued to approach the cat. "I'm sorry big guy, but I needed you. I took care of you, and now you did me, us, a great favor." Roger picked up his feline companion. Yoda flexed his claws. "Easy buddy." Suddenly the cat appeared to recognize his master and calmed down. "There you go, boy. That's my buddy," Roger said in a more relaxed tone. He had feared, for a moment, that something had gone amiss, that in the transportation process Yoda had been injured, damaged somehow, fried in the brain or something. He breathed a sigh of relief as the cat relaxed in his embrace. "Good boy, good boy," Roger stroked the cat over and over, repeating himself.

"Well, ol' boy," he finally said, lifting the cat to look into his eyes, "let's get you looked at and make sure all is okay. But first…" Roger set the cat on top of the control panel and flicked off his video equipment. He then shut down the transporter and the power supply. Yoda sat on top of the control console, bathing himself with his long tongue. Roger picked up the phone that sat on the desk adjacent to the control panel. He dialed a familiar number. "Guess what!" Roger blurted before the person on the other end even had a chance to say hello.

"Rog, is that you? Roger?" The female voice said.

"Yeah, yeah," Roger said, "it's me, and you aren't going to believe this!"

"Believe what?" The voice said.

"I sent Yoda through," Roger said nonchalantly.

There was a long pause, and then the female voice finally asked, "Yoda, the cat?"

"Yes, Yoda my cat," Roger said, in a slightly irritated tone, "what other Yoda do you know?"

"And?"

"And," Roger replied, "he's okay."

Another long silence. "Roger, I thought...well, I thought we agreed. Everyone at the office, I mean, well, Doctor Marshall—"

"Screw Doctor Marshall!" Roger broke in. "I built the damn machine, and I'll send any damn thing I want to through! It, I mean, well...hon...I'm sorry. It's just that, well, I'm excited and I thought...I thought you would be too."

"Dear," the female voice said softly, "sweetheart, I'm thrilled, and I'm sorry. I just, well, you know me. I worry. I ah—"

"I know, I know," Roger said in a more jovial tone. "I'm sorry for blowing up. I guess I'm tired and I'm just glad that Yoda made it through okay. You know what we need? A celebration. What do you say I take you to dinner tonight?"

"Rog, it's almost midnight."

Roger looked down at his watch. "Oh," he mused, "I'm sorry. Ah, how about tomorrow night?"

"Tomorrow night is great."

"Good," Roger replied. "Good. Tomorrow night."

"Roger? Rog, are you sure the cat is okay? Did you get it all on tape?"

"Yeah, yeah," he replied, "I got it."

"Well, great, darling, great. Honey, I love you." There was a click.

Roger looked at the dead receiver. "Ha, she loves me!"

He replaced the receiver and picked up the feline. He was examining the cat more thoroughly as the woman he had just spoken with made another call.

***

"The bastard did it," she said, after a male voice said hello.

"Oh, really?" the male voice said in a dull, flat voice.

"Yes," the female voice said, "he sent that damn cat of his through and apparently it worked fine."

"Great," the male voice mused. "Well, it's time for phase two of our plan."

"Thank goodness," the female voice spat, "if I have to sleep with that prick one more time…"

"Whoa, whoa, Sweet Cheeks," the male voice laughed, "you will be well compensated. And from now on you will only be bedded by me. Bye, bye." The male voice terminated the call.

***

"Who was that?" the beautiful young woman said as she plopped down on the bed next to the man as he hung up the phone.

"A bitch at work. A worthless bitch." He laughed as he cupped the young woman's breast roughly in his left hand and used her hair to pull her back onto the bed with his right. "A little bitch, just like you," he hissed, smiling. He forced his mouth down onto the young woman's, and she squealed in delight.

***

The female caller slid in between the sheets, thinking gleefully of how surprised Roger would be in just a few days.

What she did not know was that at that very moment Roger was already quite surprised. During his examination, he found that Yoda's scrotum was fine and healthy. This was surprising because, before the transportation, Yoda had no scrotum. Yoda had been cut, castrated.

***

The female voice belonged to Helen Richardson, and the male voice was that of Dr. Winston Marshall. Both were employed by the Department of Defense; however, both had their own interests and their own agendas. Winston had suggested that Helen keep a close eye on Roger and keep him posted on Roger's progress with the particle beam transporter. Helen, on the other hand, just wanted Winston, his money, and a better life than what she could afford at G.S. Level 11 and never mind that Winston already had a wife. Helen was willing to do whatever it took to get Roger to turn over the secrets to his work. Winston was also willing to do whatever it took, including killing Roger.

His methods and motives were neither known nor sanctioned by the D.O.D. As a matter of fact, the D.O.D. actually knew little of Roger's work or progress, but Dr. Marshall had known early on that Roger was on to something. He kept Roger's successes under his hat and turned in reports stating that, while Roger's work was very promising, it was in the theoretical stage only and would take many months, if not years, to reach a useful level. Roger was a nerd. He didn't care about the fame or fortune, he only cared about the research and the success of the experiments.

"And now," Winston whispered to himself, as he lay naked next to his pretty young assistant, "I will have it, and I will use it for my own designs." Winston rose from the bed. The hotel room was cheap, but it would serve him well. The young assistant had rented the room and

Winston had snuck in. "We have to be careful," he told the girl, "my wife, you know." The truth was Winston's wife had long known of his illicit affairs, of which there had been many. She had also long ago stopped caring. Winston had another reason for stealth.

He showered, dressed, and then removed a .38 special from his bag. He forced a pillow down on top of the sleeping young lady's head. She squirmed slightly. He then placed the muzzle of the gun to the pillow and pulled the trigger. The report was muffled, but louder than Winston had thought it would be. The girl's dying body quivered for a few seconds and then went limp, still.

Winston moved to the window and looked out. No movement. "Good," he said out loud. He removed the pillow. A neat hole had been drilled through the back of her beautiful young head, but most of her face was gone, taken when the bullet had exited. The air in the room was becoming foul with the smell of blood, urine, and feces. Winston slipped the gun into his pocket and left the room, locking the door behind him. He wasn't too careful, he didn't need to be. Before morning he would have what he wanted, and he would pin the murder on someone else. "Roger," he chuckled. But first, he had to go see Helen. He looked down at the .38 as he walked toward his car, which he'd parked three blocks away. "Two more times," he smiled, "two more times."

***

"Yoda, what the hell happened to you, boy?" Roger mused, as he examined the cat. "You got your manhood back, aren't *you* the lucky one." Roger stroked the cat as he reached for a headset that sported a number of magnifying glasses. He slipped the apparatus on like a ball cap and flipped one of the medium range magnifying lenses down over his right eye. "I know you're not going to like this, old boy," Roger said, "but I've got to have a look at this." Roger examined Yoda's nether regions. "No scars, it's as if..." Roger then spent the better part of two hours examining a reassembled Yoda, the machine and the videotape. It all seemed good.

"Yoda," Roger smiled, "you appear to be the first success. Well, there was the dog..." Roger had sent a lot of things through the transporter. Spoons, forks, a belt, all sorts of inanimate objects, they all moved through the transportation process quite well. It was when he attempted to send a living thing through that he had problems. He'd started with a plant, which had gone through fine, but when he'd graduated to animals, well, let's just say, the results were not so good. He'd tried to send through mice, lots of mice, about fifty. None had reappeared, not one single mouse. The coordinates of the transporter were set to only send the traveler a few feet from the booth to the carpeted platform, but each time the mice dematerialized in the booth, and never reappeared on the carpet. Roger had to assume one of two things, either they had materialized somewhere else, or they had been vaporized in hyperspace, he was just not sure.

The 'living factor' as he had begun to term it, was puzzling. Why could rings, keys, plants, anything but an animal, go through? Atoms were atoms. But the mice, Roger had suspected the problem might lie in the mice themselves, something about their genetic makeup. It was then he'd found an old stray dog and sent it through. The dog had made it. Roger's theory seemed correct, but before he'd had a chance to examine the dog, Helen had entered his lab. The dog bolted through the open door into the alley and was gone. Yoda became his only alternative.

Roger was looking again at the cat's regenerated area when the door opened. The sudden movement startled Yoda. The big cat twisted in Roger's grip, clawing his wrist in the process. The scratch was deep, and blood began to drip onto the sleeve of Roger's lab coat. "Damn cat," he hissed as he pulled off the magnifying harness. "Bad kitty!"

"Bad kitty is right," a female voice said from behind Roger, startling him. He turned to see not just Helen, but Dr. Marshall as well. Entering like they did upset him greatly, but what bothered Roger worse was that the Doctor had a gun pointed right at his chest. A bright flash erupted from the barrel of the revolver, and a deafening roar rocked the lab. Roger felt a burning sensation in his chest, and his knees went weak. The last thing he remembered was Helen and Winston dragging him toward the transporter, laughing. He knew one thing for sure, he was dying and dying fast.

***

Roger awoke slowly. Where was he? What had happened? He remembered...Yoda. Where was Yoda? Dr. Marshall! Helen? They had shot him and laughed while they shoved his dying body into the transporter. Helen had betrayed him. "She said she loved me," Roger whispered.

"Ah, love," a voice said. Roger flinched, a bit startled. He was lying in a bed constructed of logs and big sticks. The walls of the room were limestone, and the floor was slate. A single open window was set back into the wall. The room was furnished with the bed Roger was laying in, a very primitive looking bed-side stand and a longer table that sat in the middle of the room. At the table sat the man who had spoken. Roger rose on one arm.

"You are awake," the man observed. Roger's head had begun to clear. The man that sat at the simple wooden table was not old, he was ancient. He wore a long dark blue garment that ran from his neck to his ankles. The robe hosted a giant, turned-up collar. On his ancient head, he wore a hat, made of the same material as the robe, that fit loosely and tapered to a point. He wore no shoes. A great white beard ran well past his waist, and if he had hair on his aged head, it was tucked under the funny looking cap.

"Where am I?" Roger asked, as he sat up in the bed. *No pain,* he thought. *I should be in pain, I was just shot in the chest.* He looked down at himself. He wore a long crisp white nightshirt that was not his. He tore it open, no hole, no scar. "How?" Roger gasped. "Who?"

"Questions, question, questions," the old man chuckled. "Who, what, when, where, and of course, the most difficult, why? Who, first," the old man said with laughing eyes. "I am *I,* and you are *you.* What happened? I don't know, you were injured. When? Two weeks ago, well, two weeks by your time. Where? At that primitive place you call a lab. And of course, why? Why, why, why, you people always want to know why. Why? I do not know why. No one knows why. Things happen, it's not for you and me to know why.

"Your science, if that is what you want to call those infantile tinkerings you perform, always has to know the *why.* It is, you know, where you, your people, skewed off. The *why* is unimportant. Why does a seed grow? Why do birds fly south? Why does moss grow on the north side of a tree? It's not important why. That's not science. That, young man, is your feeble attempt to try and explain the unexplainable because you believe if you can explain it, you can control it, when in fact, to control it, you *can't* explain it. You have to accept it, accept it without question. For example, why are you here? Why doesn't matter. You are here, that is enough."

Roger lay back on the bed. The old man was right. Roger had spent much of his life trying to find out why, and where had it gotten him?

"Okay," Roger said, as he sat up again, "who are you and where are we?"

"Now those are proper questions," the old man said showing a row of perfect white teeth. The teeth looked out of place. "My name is Cedrick, well, it's not my real name, but you could not pronounce my real name. Where you are is, well, it's your lab, sort of. It's hard to explain. You actually did not go anywhere. You are still in your lab. You see...."

The old man told Roger a long and wild tale. Cedrick had been human many years ago or many years in the future, "depending on how you look at it," he chuckled. His civilization existed on a land mass that was no longer on the globe, or would not be for many millennia to come. Cedrick had been a scientist, of a sort. He, like Roger, had chosen a life of pure research and had ultimately sequestered himself far from his people, here, in this place.

"Speaking of which," Roger asked, "where is this place? You said it was my lab."

"It is," Cedrick replied. "You see, you grow up believing the world is this way and that way, but, in fact, it is wonderfully different, with uncountable possibilities. Have you ever been walking along and all of a sudden things looked different?" Roger nodded. "But you look desperately for something familiar. You force yourself back to that which you know, that which is acceptable, that part of the realm where you know the *why*. This place is outside the why."

"Another dimension?" Roger questioned.

Cedrick laughed. "No, no, no, boy! You are wrong-headed! Look, imagine a large castle…a large house, and you live in two rooms, but the house has thousands, tens of thousands of rooms. Just because you haven't been to those rooms doesn't mean they don't exist. And just because you don't know how to get there…" At Roger's bewildered look, Cedric gave up. "Look, you're on earth, that's all."

"So, I got here through the particle beam transporter. It transported me here?" Roger queried.

"After a fashion. Your toy," he chuckled, "allows you entry into this room of the big house. Son, it's not really a particle beam transporter. You opened a door. I just sent it all back to you." Cedrick's eyes looked amused.

"The mice?" Roger questioned.

"The mice. Wh- *why*?" Cedrick mocked.

"*What* happened to the mice?" Roger said, correcting himself.

"You are a quick learner. I eat them," Cedrick said, in a matter of fact manner, "whole and alive. Watch this," he said. He pointed to the table and, with a flash, a cat appeared. It was Yoda.

"Yoda!" The cat arched it's back as Cedrick stroked it, then leaped off the table and jumped up on Roger's bed. Roger looked at the big cat's scrotum as he picked it up.

"That's a nasty business," Cedrick said, knowing what Roger was looking for. "I can't believe you people do that, cutting off something's manhood."

"That's wh-" Roger started, and then corrected himself. "*You* restored Yoda's balls."

"Yes," Cedrick replied. "Now, watch," Cedrick pointed at the table again. Another flash of light and a dog appeared. He pointed again and, flash, it disappeared. A spoon, a fork, gold, silver, a glass of water, a rock from the moon—at least Cedrick said it was from the moon—a snake, a set of keys. "You see, I can produce all I want and all I need, except mice."

"Wh— That is peculiar," Roger mused. "I have hundreds of them at my lab."

"I know," Cedrick smiled, "and I thank you for it. You see, I need mice or rats to survive. I can get by, but it's hard. What prevents me from producing them, I don't know, but I can't." Roger lay back on the bed. He remembered his wound.

"You healed me?" Roger asked. Cedrick nodded. "Why—I know, don't ask why. How long have I been gone? I mean, have I been gone from the lab for two weeks like you said?"

"Well," Cedrick began, "you've been here two weeks, but you can go back to the exact second you left."

"Cedrick, can you transform and transport yourself?"

"Sure," Cedrick chuckled, "but once again, why would I?"

Roger laughed out loud. "We don't ask *why*, Cedrick!" Roger laughed deeper. He had forgotten how to laugh, the years in the lab had made him a recluse. "Tell you what, you do something for me, and I will do something for you."

"Why would I do that?" Cedrick's eyes lit up.

"Ah, no, no, no, Cedrick, we don't ask *why*."

***

A flash of light appeared above the small carpeted stand. A split second later Roger appeared. Helen and Winston were quite shocked. Not only was Roger apparently healed, but he was also oddly dressed. He wore a long blue robe with a pointed hat. "Roger!" Helen gasped.

Winston raised the gun and pointed it at Roger's chest. He pulled the trigger, but instead of a deafening roar, there was only a crisp click. He squeezed again, click. Click. Click. Winston lowered the gun. "What the—?"

"Well, well, well," Roger mused, as he stepped from the platform, "it's been a long time."

"What do you mean, a long time?" Helen spat. "We shot you just a few minutes ago, and now you're fine, and where did you get those silly clothes? You are—" Roger pointed his finger at Helen. Suddenly she was gone, and a white mouse appeared in her place. It was a typical white mouse, except that it was huge by mouse standards, though Roger didn't want it too big, otherwise Cedrick couldn't swallow it.

"What the hell?!" Winston ejected. Roger scooped the mouse up and placed her in a cage. He then set about collecting all the other mice, placing them in groups of twenty or so in large cages. Winston wanted to move, he wanted to kill Roger, again, but all he could do was watch, held fast by some unseen force. When Roger had finished stacking the cages onto the platform, he pointed at Winston and the strange power that had held the doctor was lifted.

"Winston, old boy," Roger began, "the young girl you killed? Oh, yes, I know about that." Winston looked shocked. His shock turned into horror as Roger continued. "Anyway, the police know of it too. I have pinned some other crimes on you as well. You will be tried, found guilty, and publicly humiliated. And, well," Roger winked at him, "I'll check in on you from time to time in your cold gray cell." Winston could hear sirens outside and car doors slamming in the alley.

"Police!" a voice yelled. "Open up!" A pounding sounded at the lab door.

"Gotta go, Winston," Roger laughed. He raised his hand as if to snap his fingers.

"But why? Why *me*?" Winston whined.

Roger stopped in mid-movement, cocked his head and smiled. "Never ask *why*, you silly man."

And with that, Roger was gone.

The End

Special thanks to Aphelion Ezine for first publication of this story in 2004.

THAT'S THREE

I walked faster as I passed the old house. I dared a quick glance. It was dark. Of course it was dark, no one lived there now. Hedges and vines protected the perimeter, setting absolute boundaries no one would have wanted to cross.

I had crossed over a time or two, perhaps three. Beneath the spreading limbs of massive live oaks and behind the mammoth hedge lay a botanist's paradise. A plethora of flora thrived inside the thorny walls, a garden, a shrine, a tribute to one man's love of God's creation.

Old Joe held a Ph.D. in botany, though he had never *worked* in the profession, at least not in the modern sense of the word. He'd never been *paid* as a professor of botany, but work he did, fervently. He lived it, breathed it. Botany consumed his entire being, seeped from his very pores. He was a man possessed by plants. Plants, and bells.

For under the secretive canopy hung a vast collection of bells made of brass, iron and even silver. They hung from trees, and they hung under the eaves of the porch. Some, the larger ones, stood proudly displayed in stands Old Joe had built himself. And once a year, at precisely midnight on New Year's Eve, he'd ring them all. Oh, what a racket.

"Plants and bells. That's what Old Joe's about," my dad always said. "He's fruity and dingy, what a waste. He's got a doctorate, for goodness' sake, and all he's done with it is pine away inside that yard." My dad had something else to say about old Joe. "Son, he's a war hero. He lost that leg at Normandy. No matter what, we owe him respect for that."

Old Joe lived with his mother in their big old house until she died, and then he lived alone—except for his plants and his bells. We, the Norths, were his closest neighbors. The Old River Road ran west out of town, past Joe's place, past our place, and right up to the river. My people had lived on the place 'since the river came in,' so my grandpa used to say.

At one time the North Bridge spanned the water, and the road continued on. The bridge was washed away in a flood in '48 or '49—I never could remember. It had happened long before my time, and there was little evidence now that a bridge had ever been there, just a dead end road blocked by a big metal gate about fifty yards past my driveway.

Anyway, it was Old Joe's mother who first caused me to cross his boundaries.

I was flying past his home on my bike that crisp November morning when I noticed her standing by the road. I wasn't sure she was his mother, I'd never seen her, but who else could she have been? There were no cars parked on the road and even though we were technically in the city limits, Old Joe's sanctuary sat several blocks apart from the closest cluster of houses.

She was just standing there, looking at the old house. Her back and bottom were wet, and the gray bun on her head had been knocked askew. She was not wearing a jacket, and her housedress was not suitable for the chilly weather. I slowed my bike as the old woman's head turned to watch me pass. She raised a feeble hand. I suppose I was somewhat distracted by the sight because I plowed into Old Joe's mailbox. I wasn't hurt, just shaken. Embarrassed, I quickly picked myself up and started to remount. Then I saw her lying on the ground.

I dropped my bike and ran across the cement road. The gate across the front walk was open. She must have gotten out. As I approached the old woman, I could smell the distinct odors of feces and urine. I gagged. "Here, ma'am," I said, gasping, "let me help you."

I grasped the old woman's outstretched hand. I pulled, and she screamed. I dropped her hand as though I'd been burned. I thought to run, to flee quickly. I actually looked around to see if anyone had seen me, but I knew if I ran someone would surely think I had assaulted her. Besides, I couldn't leave a one hundred-year-old lady lying flat on her back on the side of the road. I gagged again. "Help," I muttered unsteadily, then louder, "help, help!"

The old woman moaned. "Please help me!"

I looked around. Where in the hell was Old Joe? Perhaps he'd died in the old house. In my imagination, he was lying in the leaf-strewn, overgrown yard, just past the thorny hedge. "Oh, crap," I groaned. "Ma'am? Ma'am, hold on, and I'll get your son."

"My son," she murmured. "You *are* my son. Joseph, help me now."

"Ah, ma'am, just hold on."

I ran through the gate—and into another world. The yard was beyond neat, it was *meticulous*. I knew what Alice felt when she went through the looking glass. Small, clearly defined areas were dedicated to different types of flora, each clearly marked with a hand-painted sign. Even though it was November, not a single fallen leaf littered the sculpture Old Joe had created. It took my breath. My steps slowed as I tried to take it all in, but then I remembered the old lady. I could hear her moaning, though I could no longer see her through the thick hedge. As I hurried up the walk, I noticed something I never had, though I'd passed the house a thousand times. There was a fence on the inside of the hedge.

I ran up on the porch and pounded on the door. "Ah, Old—" I started to yell 'Old Joe.' "Oh, shit." I thought furiously. What the hell was his last name? "Anybody home?" I screamed instead. There was no answer. "You're dead, aren't you, you old bastard?" I muttered to myself. "You're dead in there, and your old mammy is lying out on the cold ground." How in the hell did I get myself into this? Then it hit me. His last name was Belts. Mr. Belts. After all, it was on the mailbox I had just run into. "Hey, Mr. Belts, you home? Your mom, she's hurt!" I waited a moment, silently hoping. "Shit."

I ran toward the back of the house along a little gravel path. Next to the old place was a greenhouse, a little house entirely made of glass. I never knew it was there. A light! The place was lit up! "Mr. Belts!" I yelled again. I was so enamored by the little crystal cottage, I didn't realize Old Joe was standing in the path in front of me.

"What?" His voice boomed across the yard, and I nearly wet my pants. "What in the hell do you want, boy?"

"Ah, ah, Mr. Belts, I mean Dr. Belts," I remembered that if you held a Ph.D. you were to be addressed as Doctor. At twelve I wasn't sure why that was, but it seemed to soften the old coot. "Ah, sir, it's your mom! Your mother! She's out front, hurt!"

"Oh no!" The old man's face went white. He shoved quickly past me and hobbled toward the open gate.

I teetered and nearly fell over one of the large stones lining the walkway, but with a monumental effort, I managed to keep my balance. To have planted one foot off the designated path would surely have damned me to a fate worse than death. No keep off the grass signs were needed. I regained my composure and ran to join him.

Old Joe sank down on his good knee. "Mother! Mother, what happened?" At her silence, he turned to me. "Boy! What happened? Do you know?"

"Well, uh, she fell, I-I guess. I was on the road and, ah…she fell."

He turned back to the fallen woman. "Mother, hold on, I'll get help. Son, stay with her. I'll call an ambulance."

He rose and shuffled off toward the house. He moved quickly for an eighty-year-old man with a wooden leg. He was gone maybe two minutes, but it seemed to me like two days. I knelt next to the old woman to try and comfort her. I nearly threw up. I'm sure I was an odd shade of green by the time he returned with a blanket.

"I called the ambulance. Can you help me cover her up?"

"Ah, yes! Yes, sir."

We tucked the blanket around her body, but I could already hear the sirens. The fire station was on our side of town, so they only had a few blocks to travel. I watched quietly as the paramedics loaded the old woman into the rig, then I turned and walked toward my bike. A big hand gripped my shoulder and spun me around. For the second time in just a few minutes, I nearly wet myself.

"You're one of Billy North's grandsons, aren't you. You are?" Old Joe stared solemnly down at me, awaiting my answer.

"Uh, Edward, sir. William North is my grandpa."

"Well, thank you," he said gravely. "Thank you very much. You probably saved my mother's life. I, ah…I've got to go. I have to follow the ambulance."

"In a car?" I blurted.

"Yes, son, of course."

It never occurred to me that the old hermit could drive, let alone own an automobile.

"That's two," he said.

"Two, sir?"

"You saved my mother. Years ago Billy saved me, right over there." He pointed down the road toward the river. "I was on that bridge the night it was washed away. Your Grandpa Billy pulled me from the wreckage."

Old Joe turned and hobbled away. I watched as the ambulance pulled off. A short moment later a bright, shiny blue Chevrolet appeared mysteriously from a gap in the hedge. It was a gate, of course. The car stopped, and Old Joe emerged. He closed the secret exit, then climbed back into the car and drove away.

"Amazing!" I gasped. The Chevy was a fifty-seven, almost twenty years old, but it looked as though it had just been driven off the showroom floor. I stood gaping right in the middle of the road as Old Joe's taillights disappeared into the gray dusk. Then I walked over to my bike, picked it up and mounted.

"I guess I saved the old girl," I muttered. I felt pretty good. Then I noticed Old Joe's mailbox had been knocked sideways. Hoping he would forgive me, I pedaled off into the twilight.

***

That was five years ago. Twice more in those five years I entered the yard. Both times it was nearly dark, and I was walking past when a voice addressed me from the hedge. "Edward North," the voice said, "come here." The first time was about a year after the 'mother incident' as it had come to be called, and the second was on my sixteenth birthday.

The first time, Old Joe took me around his sanctuary and showed me the entire set-up. I was only thirteen then, too young to fully appreciate what I was seeing. On the second occasion, my sixteenth birthday, he took me into the garage and showed me The Car. It was beautiful.

"Would you like to drive it?" he asked me, and I did. He and I rode together in The Car. I was scared to death.

After we parked, Old Joe showed me to the gate.

"Thank you Mr. Belts," I said.

"No, thank you," he replied seriously. "I had a son, once." He sighed, and his eyes held a faraway look. "He was born in Berlin during the war and was killed during the bombing."

"Oh. I didn't know you—" I stopped, unsure of what to say.

"No, no one knows." He smiled, but I could see tears forming. "I was not married to his mother. I was an American G.I. She was just a girl of eighteen. I never spoke of it, but now…" His voice grew hoarse and trailed off. "In any event," he spoke up, "I would have been proud if he had grown up like you." With that, Joe turned on his good leg and disappeared into his haven.

Later that evening, alone in my room, I heard the most awful scream, a long, piercing wail that echoed through the night. I arose quickly to seek out the source, but all in my home were fast asleep. Perhaps it was a dream.

The next evening when I arrived home from school my grandpa informed me that Mrs. Belts had passed away in the night.

"Gone," he said. "Gone."

That was over a year ago. I remember because my seventeenth birthday came and went without incident. But the day after, one year to the day after Joe's mother's death I heard the wail again, and as if on cue, I came home to find Grandpa had more news.

"Old Joe died," he said. "Too bad."

"Well, Grandpa, what will happen to the old place now?"

Grandpa shook his head. "It's hard to say, boy, hard to say."

One month later I heard the wail again. That was three, but this time no one died. Two weeks after that I was diagnosed with a rare form of lymphatic cancer. So it was that I, at the tender age of seventeen, came face to face with my own mortality. The doctor explained that I would feel normal and strong for a while and then, well, there was small hope. He assured me new cures were coming out every day, but in his eyes I could find little comfort.

On the drive home from the doctor that day all my mother could do was rub my arm and keep repeating, "It will be okay. Somehow it will be okay."

Christmas came and went. My father and mother were handling my illness much worse than I. I felt fine, in fact, I had never felt better, though I knew I would soon waste away and die. I tried not to think about it and kept myself occupied. It was one of those preoccupations that put me in front of Old Joe's that night, the thirty-first of December.

I was returning from a new year's eve party. I hadn't stayed until midnight because I realized I might not have another year with my family and I wanted to be at home when the new year, possibly my last year, rang in. I know, seventeen years old and so melancholy, but when you are dying...

I walked faster as I passed the old house. I dared a quick glance. It was dark, of course. No one lived there now. Joe and his mom were gone. It was almost twelve and I hurried faster. I *had* to make it.

Then the bells began to ring, their strident voices loud and clear in the crisp winter air.

I was seventeen years old, a brave young man facing death, but *this?* This was something else. I started to run home, but my steps slowed as I wondered just why I was frightened. What was at home that could mean more than this? I turned and made my way back toward the old house. The bells pealed louder, rising toward a clamorous crescendo. Was it Old Joe's ghost ringing them? The thought thrilled me. Six months ago I would have been horrified, but now anticipation raced through my veins, and my skin tingled.

I put my hand on the gate and tried the latch. It was locked tight, but as I tested it again, the bells stopped abruptly. I skirted the perimeter of the yard to the point where I knew the secret gate lay, The Car exit. It was not locked, and swung open silently at the touch of my hand.

Cautiously I entered Joe's domain. It had changed little. Joe had been dead three months, but the grounds still looked tended, as though even the trees honored his memory in their reluctance to shed their leaves on the still-green grass. I ventured on toward the white gravel path.

I heard a voice, and then another. "No! Please don't!" It sounded like a young woman. "Please, I'll do *anything. Please* don't kill me." Her voice was heavily accented, German.

"Shut up, bitch," a man's voice snarled. "Why did you think I brought you here?"

My town was a small one, but I recognized neither voice. "Hey," I yelled instinctively, bursting into the open. "What the hell?" The man closed the gap between us in a second. He had a pistol, and he held it pointed at my head.

"Who are you?" he demanded, then before I could reply he added, "it don't matter. Get down on your knees!"

Knowing one is dying gives a person a certain freedom, one that few people ever really get to appreciate. "Go to hell," I spat. Was I brave or what? He slammed the revolver into the side of my head, and I went down anyway. I rolled on one side and then pushed up on my knees. "You are an idiot," I gasped, spitting blood. "You rang all those bells! Pretty soon everyone in town will be down here to see what's going on!"

"What? What bells? Boy, there were no bells ringing, at least not here." Behind him, the girl rose to run, and the man casually slammed the pistol into the side of her head. She went down, landing face first, and lay very still. He looked down at her. "We will find it *or else*." She did not respond.

"Find what?" I choked on the words, and my head was pounding.

"The money, the jewels, the gold. The treasure!"

Even in the moonlight, I could see his dark eyes sparkle. "Treasure? You ignorant son of a bitch, there's no *treasure* here! Old Joe was on a pension. He wasn't *rich*!"

"But he was! He wrote letters to Isadore, here." He waved a hand toward the unconscious girl. "He told her he had a *yard full* of buried treasure!"

Sometimes the truth comes slow, sometimes fast. This was a blinding epiphany. Joe's idea of treasure was plants, glorious green, rare, *plants*. "You're an idiot," I groaned, "you don't know!"

The man pointed the gun at the girl's head. "I will kill you both," he said coldly. "No one will hear out here." He pushed the gun against her temple. I put one foot squarely beneath me and launched myself at him. I meant to tackle him, wrestle him down, but instead he twisted the gun and fired at me. The bullet took me in the chest. Amazingly, I felt nothing. He'd missed, he must have. I plowed into the man, knocking him backward, and the gun went flying. We scrambled for it. I saw blood, lots of blood. I thought I must have injured him. My hands closed around the weapon, but his hands closed around mine. I yanked hard. The gun exploded in a burst of blue and white light. The would-be killer staggered back, most of his head gone, and fell dead.

I looked down at myself. Reddish orange blood oozed from a single hole punched in my jacket. I tore open my coat. My shirt was soaked with blood and more squirted out with every beat. Suddenly I felt weak. With every breath came a sharp shooting pain. I sank down to rest on a large rock.

After a moment the girl stirred, and then sat up. She pressed her hand to her dark blonde hair and brought it down in front of her face. Her eyes widened at the blood she saw on her fingers. She looked slowly around the yard as though she had no memory of where she was. Then she saw me. "Oh! Oh, dear heavens! Who are you? What happened?"

I pressed my hand over the hole in my chest. Blood oozed between my fingers. "He's dead," I said, nodding at the still twitching corpse, "and to answer your question, I'm just a neighbor. Eddie."

She pushed herself to her knees and crawled over beside me. "Eddie? You saved my great grandmamma! My grandpapa wrote of you!"

"Your grandpa?" Suddenly the pain in my chest intensified. I couldn't move and I couldn't breathe.

She laid her hand on my knee. "My mother was Joseph Belts' daughter. She was born and raised in Berlin."

"He spoke of a son," I gasped. My vision was dimming. The world beyond her pale face ceased to exist.

She pushed herself to her feet, wobbling for a moment. "That was mama's twin brother, he was killed when they were babies. I will get an ambulance!"

Her voice faded away. I slid off the boulder. I couldn't sit any longer. Even though the air was cold, I was suddenly very warm, and sleep beckoned me to the edge of consciousness. I was slipping off into a cozy slumber as the sirens sounded, hollow and distant to my ears. I wondered who they were for. *Some poor soul is in trouble*, I thought drowsily. Then I slipped into the dark.

When I came to myself, it was daylight. I was standing on the old river road. *How? What?* I looked up at the roof of Old Joe's house peeking through the trees, and then higher at the white puffy clouds in the azure sky. "It was a dream," I said in wonder, "a damn dream!" I looked down at my chest, ran my hands over my jacket. There was no hole. "I'm alive! I didn't get shot!"

Then I remembered the cancer. "Oh, well," I sighed.

I heard a rustle. I looked up at the hedge just as the hidden gate swung open and The Car rolled out onto the road. Old Joe sat behind the wheel. "That's three," he said, smiling. He put the shifter up into park and slid across the front seat. "You drive."

I was surprised to see him, yet comforted, pleased. I eased in behind the wheel and gave him a broad grin. He pointed down the road, and I punched the gas. The Car picked up speed as we approached my house. I noticed there were a lot of cars in the drive. I looked past them toward the gate, but it was gone and the bridge was there, rebuilt overnight!

"Looks like a wake at your place," Joe laughed. The car shifted into high as we flew past the house. By the time we hit the bridge, the speedometer was buried.

"Mr. Belts, where are we going?"

"Anywhere you want, son, anywhere you want. And Eddie? Call me Joe, Old Joe." We both laughed.

Behind us, the bridge burst into a million beautiful colors. Mom was right. Somehow it would all be okay.

The End

THE GROVE

All things, both real and imagined, have a beginning, a point in time when they were not—and then they were. So it was with the grove. Sequestered by a small clearing, yet hidden within a vast ocean of green, the Aspens of the grove huddled together, an island of white bark and golden leaves separated from the rest of the wild by happenstance...or destiny.

I wouldn't have even gone to the grove that day, but that was where the well was. And he might have been in the well.

I had heard stories of hauntings and strange lights in the night sky, but they were just old wives tales, and I didn't put much stock in them. Never the less, in the bright light of day, I had explored the grove thoroughly. Unable to find evidence that any structure had ever been built there, I finally concluded that the well had been dug for the sole purpose of watering the grove, perhaps in its infancy. *Who* dug the well was beyond my scope of knowledge, though somehow I knew it was ancient.

I tied up my horse about a quarter of a mile down the little dirt track that ran along the forest's edge. The well trained Appaloosa hated the grove, and no matter how hard I tried, I couldn't make him go near it.

The sun sank below the horizon as I walked the distance to the grove. The first autumn leaves crackling faintly under my feet were the only sounds I heard. I passed quickly through the Aspens to the small clearing in the center. Moss covered blocks of granite made a wide ring around the well and grass grew right up to it, as though no one ever walked there. I scanned the ground as I crossed to the well. There were no footprints. With some trepidation, I leaned over the rocky edge and cast my lantern light down on the water below. The black walls seemed to absorb the light, and I had to lean uncomfortably far down to see that the surface of the water was unbroken.

I stood up and looked around. Twilight had set in, and the darkened tops of the trees seemed hunched, their lower branches reaching down. I hurried outside, unwilling to admit that the haste in my steps had anything to do with the gathering gloom, but at the edge of the grove I paused and looked back. In the daylight the grove was a place of some discomfort; in the gray-blue light of dusk, discomfort matured to dread. I felt that something was going to happen. Something bad. The .44 caliber pistol I wore on my side afforded little reassurance against my rising anxiety.

I made myself stand for a moment, fighting the absurd urge to bolt back to where my horse was tied, swing up into the well-oiled saddle and urge the old Appy into a full gallop. I reasoned with myself, berating myself for acting the fool. But the grove was not a reasonable place.

I walked away, stubbornly maintaining a deliberate stride. Seventy-five more feet and I would reach the dusty track down which my horse waited. Fifty feet. Forty feet. From the corner of my eye, I saw him, just for a second. He was gone in a flash, faster than any human could move.

I spun on one heel, but there was nothing there. Was it a trick of the light? An illusion brought on by my nervousness? Had the missing boy for whom I was searching actually been there and run off? Where could he have gone that quickly?

I was unable to answer any of these questions as I held my lantern high and looked about me. I saw no bent grass, no sign of any passage other than my own. I must have imagined it. As I turned again to leave, a high pitched giggle floated out from the trees. The maniacal undertones in the chilling sound touched something primal in me, and at that moment my desire to remain in control of my fear was overcome by the urge to run. I ran. Openly and unashamedly, I ran from the grove.

As I reached the dirt track my survival instinct was finally overwhelmed by my natural curiosity. I stopped and looked back. There was movement in the small clearing around the well. Something was circling the edge of the clearing, clockwise. It was moving so fast it was really just a blur. I had never seen anything like this. I doubted anyone had. As I watched, the streak seemed to increase its speed. It went around and around, reminding me of the carousel I had seen once at the state fair—but an out of control version.

The thing was moving so fast it was hard to tell where it ended, when a blinding light burst forth from the well. At the same moment came a sound like the crack of a hundred guns, then nothing. All went silent, still and dark.

That was the beginning. Or maybe the beginning came much earlier, eons earlier. I don't know.

***

My dad was waiting on the porch when I pulled up in the yard.

"They found him."

"What?" I asked, puzzled.

"They found the McFarland kid. You know? The one you've been a' huntin'." He narrowed his eyes. "You okay, boy? You look as if you'd seen a ghost. And you've been runnin' that horse hard. What'd you do, run into a pack of injuns?" Dad laughed at that. It was 1939 and all the 'injuns' were long gone, living on reservations now. "Now I'll tell you, boy, your old granddad, *he* had some injun stories, he—"

"Uh, Dad?" At his sharp look, I apologized. "I didn't mean to interrupt you, sir, I just…"

He gave me a worried look. "You just what, son?"

"I…just… I think something startled my horse, that's all." I couldn't quite bring myself to tell him what I'd seen. "Where did they find the McFarland kid?"

"Oh, hell! Little fart fell asleep in the hayloft and then wouldn't come out when they were yellin' for 'im! Afraid of a whuppin' I expect. Needs a sight many more than what he gets in my opinion. You mark my word, that little hellion is gonna' be mean as a rattler if someone don't lay down some law over there. What are there, nine or ten of them kids? They run over their pa something fierce. Tell you what, I wouldn't put up with that, no sirree! And I'll tell you something else, I wouldn't put up with that woman he has neither!"

I smiled and let Dad's words wash over me as I climbed down from the saddle and loosened the cinch.

"You know what old Chad Withers said? I shouldn't ought to repeat it, but he said that whole bunch of kids are bastards!" I shot a sideways glance at him. "Well, he said it. Old man McFarland and his wife aren't married, no sir!"

"But Dad, I'm eighteen and ever since I can remember, they've lived together—"

"That don't make no never mind. Man and woman gots to go to the preacher and do it right. I did! Your ma and me, we went. That could explain a lot…" He rubbed his chin. "I mean, living in sin, and all…"

"Who's living in sin?" my mother asked as she stepped out on the porch.

"Those McFarlands!"

Mother furrowed her brow. "Which ones?"

"The old man and the old woman!"

"Good heavens, Sherman, who said that? *You* didn't say that, did you? Good Lord, I hope not!"

"Well, if it's true—"

She put her hands on her hips and said, "Sherman, it's *not* true. I was at their wedding. They are from over in Lincoln County. They got married in Pastor Beisley's church."

"Are you sure? Because old Chad Withers said—"

"Chad Withers is plumb full of beans! I was young, but I think—"

"See! You don't know!"

"Ah, horsefeathers…"

The conversation faded from my hearing as they went inside, and I was left alone in the yard with the Appaloosa. I pulled the saddle off the big horse and led him to the barn. I flipped on the electric lights—a relatively new addition—and led the horse into a stall. Dad kept a radio in the barn, mostly for the noise, and I flipped it on before I rubbed down the horse. The classical strains drifting softly from the speaker couldn't distract my mind from what I'd seen. Should I tell my dad? No, he'd just think I'd been drinking, not that I was much on drinking, or that I'd gone plumb loco. I decided to keep it to myself, for now.

I finished up with the horse and closed up the barn. Outside in the yard, I stopped to listen to the night. I could hear the cows in their pasture and the faint voices of Mom and Dad still arguing over the legitimacy of the McFarland children.

Underneath it all, I could still hear that giggle, and all I could think about was the grove.

***

Days grew to weeks, weeks to months and months to years. I steered clear of the grove, though several times I thought to return. But for reasons I knew not, I did not. Then a darkness came upon the world, the kind of darkness that could only be spawned in the depths of men's hearts.

World War II broke out. When Pearl Harbor was bombed, I knew I must leave Montana for places far away, perhaps never to return, except for burial. I sat alone on the porch one night, then Dad came out to join me. "Dad," I said, as I looked out across our peaceful pastures, "I have to go."

"I know, boy" he answered sadly. "I had to go, too, in my time. I was much younger than you." He looked away for a long time, the planks under his rocking chair creaking gently, then spoke again. "You'll see things...things that change a man. It's always been that way, I guess."

I spoke softly so Mom wouldn't hear. "Dad, if I don't make it back—"

"Don't even think that way! You may not even get over there!"

"Dad, if I don't get back, bury me in that grove of Aspens up on Thompson's ridge."

Dad stopped rocking and gave me a puzzled look. "Are you sure? I mean, that place..."

"Is strange?"

"Well, I would use another word, but if that's your wish... Hell, it's not even gonna' come to that. You're a fine woodsman and the best shot I know! I hate to admit it, but you're better than me! You'll do fine."

"I hope so," I said. "I hope so."

We sat in silence for a moment, then I said, "tomorrow I'm gonna' go down and volunteer."

Dad patted me on the shoulder then stood up and went into the house. In all my years that was the only time I saw him cry.

I sat for a moment longer, then went out to the barn and saddled the Appaloosa. I had to go back. We walked in darkness, the horse and I, but he seemed to know where we were going. For the first time, he trotted all the way up to the grove.

I climbed down from the saddle, still unsure why I had come. I carried a battery-powered flashlight, but the moon was bright, so I left it off. Inside, the grove seemed brighter somehow. I looked around without knowing what I was looking for. I still felt uneasy, but there was a strange sense of comfort to the grove tonight. I stepped out into the clearing in the center. It may have been a trick of the light, but it seemed that a moonbeam shone directly onto a stool sized rock. I sat down on the rock. Nothing happened.

Above me, the moon shone impassively. I stared at it, knowing that however far I went, the moon would still be the same. Feeling silly, I spoke aloud, "I'm here. Show yourself." Still, nothing happened. Perhaps I had imagined everything.

I sat for a long time, looking at the night. It was peaceful and calm, though a bit too quiet. As I rose to leave a movement to my right caught my eye. I reached for my flashlight, then decided not to disturb the darkness. I walked to my horse, picked up the reins and prepared to mount. A soft, warm breeze caressed my face, and a voice behind me whispered, "You will return. I will see to it." I spun around, and this time I used the flashlight. There was no one there.

I flipped off the light and climbed on my horse. "We will see," I said. I turned the big horse toward home. I finally knew why I had gone to the grove. I had to overcome my fear.

That night was the beginning. I had a lot of fear to overcome, and I was right about going far. I went all the way to the beaches of Normandy on D-Day.

***

I survived the landing, but I didn't think I would survive the night. The barrage of German artillery was deafening. I had slept on the ground before, but this was different. This was a night of death preceded by a day of death. I'd watched a lot of my buddies fall, and a lot of guys I didn't know fall, too. An eighteen-year-old kid died in my arms. I still had his blood on my sleeve. The only prayer I still bothered with was that they would ship my body state-side. I did not want to be buried in this God-forsaken land, to rest eternally amongst people who were not my own.

Hunkered down below a German-built rampart, I scribbled these words on an envelope that contained a letter from my mother: If I fall, please return my remains to my family in Montana. I signed my name, followed by my serial number. I hoped it would be enough. I had no sooner tucked the note back in my pocket when the battalion commander tapped me on the shoulder.

"Got another one, kid?"

"Another what?"

"Another cig. Didn't you just light one?"

"Oh, ah, no sir. I mean, here, sir, I've got a pack. I, ah, I wasn't lighting up…" I handed him the pack, and he tapped one out.

"Lost mine," he said. "I don't know where. Probably in the drink. Blasted sea water. You ever seen anything like this?" He didn't wait for an answer. "Hell no you ain't, no one has! Boy, they are chopping us up like horse shit in a coffee grinder. Damn those Kraut bastards!" He drew on the cigarette and exhaled with a grimace. "Oh hell, boy, you know they're just like us—scared shitless. Who the hell thinks up this kinda' crap? You bet your ass they ain't *here*. Hell no, they sent you and me. I found the Lieutenant Colonel. He was hit by machine-gun fire. 'Bout cut in half." He held up the lighter he had just used. "Didn't seem like he'd need this again. If we get home, maybe I can give it to his son.

"The Major's dead too, and that puts me in charge. We can't stay here. We're going up the hill in forty-five minutes. It's gonna' cost us, but we'll lose a lot more if we stay. Are you okay, kid?"

"Yes, sir, Captain. It's just been a long night—and a long day too."

"Yeah, it's something." He shivered. "And cold, too."

"Well, I'm from Montana, sir. Cold, I can stand."

"Ah, Big Sky country. I'm a Texan born, but I've been up in Colorado for a lot of years. That's how I wound up here. I was in the Reserves at Fort Carson. Next thing you know, I'm on active duty and over here. What about you?"

"I volunteered."

"No kidding! Well, bless your heart. You've got balls, boy."

"Well, sir, I felt it was the right thing to do."

Just then a huge German shell exploded not one hundred yards away.

"Crap and corruption! We've got to quiet those guns! Well, boy, I've got to go. Pass it up the line. Forty-five minutes, we are over the hill."

With that, he was gone. I looked around, but there was no line to pass it on to. My line was gone, dead, except for me. Forty-five minutes. I could stay put, but it wouldn't be right. Besides, I figured I had as good a chance of getting it here as I did there. I looked at my watch ninety times every thirty seconds. It was the longest forty-five minutes of my life. I waited and watched, and finally we moved.

Our battalion ran up over the hill, guns flashing. I fired and ran and ran and fired. I saw the Captain once or twice. I killed at least a dozen men for sure, maybe more. I rounded a small mound, and the ground exploded in front of me in a neat line. I had nearly run into a machine-gun nest.

Instinctively I dropped to the ground. I fell on something, someone.

"Hey, Montana, that you?"

"Captain?"

"Yeah, kid, it's me."

"You okay, sir?"

"Yeah. I'm hit, but I'm all right. Stay down. Hey, I found my cigs." He laughed. "They were in my gunny sack. A shell tore through it, cut it right in half! I looked down and damn, there they were. Go figure."

"Are you sure you're okay, Captain?"

"Hell yeah, kid, I'm fine. I just caught some shrapnel in the leg. It's stopped bleeding now. I've had worse. Yeah, I'll probably get the Heart. Hell, I've already got two. You hit, kid?"

"No, sir, I don't think so. It's…"

"Scary. We gotta' take out that nest. You got any grenades?"

"Yes, sir!"

"Well, lets chunk a few over there."

I rose up to throw. One…two… Then out of nowhere a German soldier appeared and fired at me, point blank, just as I threw the third grenade. I felt the bullet tear through my shoulder and then another creased my skull. I saw the third grenade explode in the nest. Their ammo went up with it. For an eerie moment the world was all aglow. I saw the muzzle flash from the Captain's .45 caliber pistol once, twice, then a third and fourth time. I watched as in slow motion the young German's head disappeared, blown away by the slugs from the 1911. My knees were weak. I collapsed, and the Captain grabbed me.

"Oh hell, kid, you're hit!"

"That's not my blood, sir," I said groggily. "That's from some kid earlier. It's not mine."

"Kid! Kid!" I could hear the Captain shouting. "Dammit, Montana, hold on! Ah, damn, kid."

The Captain's voice echoed softly in my mind, as though it came from a far distance. I couldn't figure out why he was still yelling when I was so far away. I was tired. It was dark, and I wanted to rest. *Kid, don't close your eyes!* Was the Captain still shouting? The front of my shirt was wet and sticky. Must have spilled something...boy, would Ma be mad...better get in and change...

The old Appy was waiting. My shirt wasn't so bad. I didn't really have anything better to do, and he was pawing the ground, ready to go. I wondered where Ma and Daddy were. Oh, well, it didn't matter.

Kid hold on! I heard yelling and lots of loud noise, but then it faded away. I climbed on the horse. The cool Montana breeze felt good on my face. The horse turned on his own and headed down the road. I heard Daddy behind me, yelling for the horse to stop. I tried to stop it, but it broke into a run, galloping down the old dirt track and right up to the grove.

I heard no more loud noises, but I knew Daddy and someone else were looking for me. I couldn't go back, I had to get into the grove. I swung down from the saddle. Strangely, my shirt was wet again. Stranger still, there was someone in the grove. It was a girl, no, a woman.

She was young, eighteen or nineteen, and dressed in a long white gown. The gown was transparent, revealing a well-proportioned figure, and long blonde hair flowed past her shoulders and down her back, framing an angelic face. I knew she couldn't be from around here. She looked at me, and a loud trumpet blast sounded. This was all new. I had never heard any sounds or seen anyone in the grove before.

"I told you I'd see you returned." She raised her chin defiantly. "See, I'm true to my word. I never lie—well, *almost* never." She giggled. Her voice was impish, as well as her laughter, and I found myself smiling at her as she continued. "This is your place, your destiny."

"My destiny?" Despite the explanation she offered, I was still confused at how I had come here. "What's going on? I was somewhere else. There was a lot of noise, explosions... Guns! Guns were going off." I walked toward the woman, but she vanished, reappearing on the rock I had sat on before I left.

Something caught my eye, and I turned away from her to look at the well. A beam of black light rose from the depths. It looked just like the beam from my flashlight, but instead of brilliant white, it was black as pitch, narrow at the bottom and widening as it rose skyward. "What the hell?"

"Hell is right," she giggled. "It's Hell and Hell it will be!" She smoothed the front of her gown in a sensual gesture and giggled again. "Don't pay any attention to it. As long as the flow is black, all is well with this door. Of course, if the flow is speckled, well, oops, better watch out, all Hell is breaking loose! Away they will go to be bad, bad, bad!

"But you want to stay with me, don't you? We can have great fun. I am very tired of being alone. We can play in the grove, you and me, me and you, all day long! Stay with me, please? Please, please?"

I shook my head, confused, and stammered, "I, I...uh..."

"You can kiss me," she offered, and winked. "You can--"

"Hey, what do you mean, 'if the flow is speckled'?"

"Oopsy, poopsy." She laughed, and then said, "then I gotta' tell."

"Tell who?"

"The guardians. You know, the big bad boys." She stiffened her shoulders and stomped her feet in an imitation of a military march. "Then it's big trouble for sure."

The truth of the place was slowly penetrating my foggy mind. I turned to tell her I should go, when she spoke again.

"Saw you when you came looking for that kid. He wasn't here, no sirree. No one's here, much. A long time ago," giggle, giggle, "I had a friend. He's gone down there." She pointed at the well. "Goodbye, so long, so sad." She looked at me solemnly, but I could see the amusement in her eyes. "But *you* can stay. I won't let them take *you*. You are strong. I saw you when you came back—no fear. Stay, what do you say? Stay here."

She stood and glided toward me. Her presence was alluring. "Kiss me and stay." Her voice had deepened to a sultry purr, and I felt myself moving closer to her.

"Damn horse!"

The voice boomed like a hundred cannons behind me. I spun around. My dad stood next to the Appaloosa. His mare waited nearby while he fixed a halter on the Appy. He looked up and his eyes met mine.

"Son! Son is that you...are you there kid!" Blinding light flashed in my eyes. "Dammit, Montana!" the Captain bellowed. "Damn your hide, don't you dare do that again. I thought for sure you were gone!" He looked up at someone beyond my sight. "Get this hero the hell out of here, now! He knocked out that nest and took a round for me too!" He looked back down at me and said, "boy, I thought you were gone."

The medics laid me on a stretcher. One of them looked at the Captain and gasped. "Captain, you're hit! You are going, too!"

"To hell I am!" he responded. Just then his legs went out from under him. "Oh, all right," he grumbled from the ground.

A second pair of medics appeared and with just a little protest got him laid back on another stretcher. His injuries were worse than he had let on, but he and I both survived. Unlike a lot of other good men, we made it home.

***

I had been home for two weeks when I did it. I was just leaving the house when Dad came up to me.

"Where are you going, boy?"

"I have some unfinished business, Dad."

"At the grove?"

"Yes, sir," I stammered. "Ah—"

"You know, I seen a young man I thought was you one day when that cantankerous horse of yours got out. I guess I was just hallucinating."

"Probably so." I chuckled. "Old age will do that."

"Do you hurt much?"

"Naw, dad, the bullet passed right on through. I was blessed."

I arrived home late, that night. Dad sat on the porch. After I put up the horse, I pulled up a chair and sat next to him.

"Funny thing, son, but I would swear I heard a blast like dynamite just before sundown."

I shrugged. "Maybe someone finally blew that old well."

"That'd be a good thing. It wasn't worth much, no-how. A young girl got thrown down there when I was a boy. Drowned. A well like that is better off sealed." He wrinkled his nose and sniffed the air. "You smell something? Smoke?"

"It's probably Aspens burning. You know, it's that time of year, big bonfires and all."

Ma stuck her head out the door. "War's over! They just said it on the radio!"

Dad clapped me on the shoulder. "Let's celebrate! It's a great day!"

I smiled at him. "A great day indeed."

The End

Special thanks to Bewildering Stories Ezine for first publication of The Grove in 2007

ABOUT THE AUTHOR

Ezra T. Gray grew up in a small town in the mid-south where he was born again at the age of eleven while attending an old-fashioned Pentecostal Revival. While the road may have been rocky, he has always maintained his relationship with Jesus Christ. After graduating high school, he joined the military. He attended John A. Logan College and Southern Illinois University, majoring in Criminal Justice and Administration of Justice. He has since spent his time working in various positions related to that field.

In his travels Ezra visited many exotic locations and has crossed the United States from coast to coast, living in places as far apart as Maine and Alaska.

Ezra has many varied interests. He is a 32nd-degree Mason, an ordained minister, a black belt in Judo and a firearms instructor. He is also a dedicated Biblical scholar, studying scripture three times a day without fail.

Writing has always been one of his passions. He began writing short stories years ago for friends and subsequently had some published. He has several published novels and a collection of short stories.

OTHER WORKS BY EZRA T. GRAY

Camp of The Saints:
The Journey Begins (Book One)

Darkness has fallen...

The Great Tribulation has come. America—and the world—is ruled by an anti-Christian government. Nephilim again walk the earth and chimeras roam like packs of feral dogs.

There was no pre-Tribulation rapture, and most Christians were unprepared for The Tribulation. Only a small percentage of the world's Christian population remains and those left have only three choices: take the Mark of the Beast, die, or run.

But there are lights in the darkness...

In a small cabin in the Rocky Mountain wilderness, one young warrior faces down a pack of chimeras and meets some unlikely allies. Guided by God and assisted by angels, this small band of determined Christians prepares for a journey so important even the Devil himself is determined to stop them.

Available on Amazon in paperback or Kindle edition.

Hell has come 'a calling—
but Hell has never met Mac McGreggor

THE BEELZEBUB
FACTOR

NEPHILIM RESURRECTED BOOK ONE

EZRA T. GRAY

The Beelzebub Factor

Mac McGreggor is a Marine turned demon hunter. He spends his time helping those who have nowhere else to turn. When an old friend calls for help, a series of events is set into motion that draws Mac into a conspiracy thousands of years in the making.

Beelzebub is a desperate demon with an agenda. He is running out of time and he knows he needs the one man he can't sway. As the pendulum swings, Beelzebub offers Mac a deal—one he won't let Mac refuse.

Estranged brothers reunited…

An underground facility with horrifying secrets…

New vows tested…

Old alliances betrayed…

With Beelzebub holding all the cards, Mac is left with a hopeless choice—allow Beelzebub to unleash the unholy race of Nephilim, or risk his life and the lives of his family and friends in an all-out battle against the Prince of Hell himself.

Will Mac prevail or will the Nephilim rule?

Available on Amazon in paperback or Kindle edition.

Camazotz Millennium

Shot down over the South American jungle, Buddy MacBelle is captured by rebels, tortured, and held as a POW. His chance to escape finally arrives, but very quickly he realizes that rebels are not the most dangerous things in the jungle.

In a long forgotten pyramid, an ancient evil is stirring. Bloodthirsty creatures known as Camazotz are organizing and massing for an assault of global proportions.

Following a confrontation inside the pyramid, where he took shelter after escaping the rebels, Buddy again escapes with nothing but his life. During the fight, though, he discovers there is something special about him—something the Camazotz fear.

Years later, the incident in the jungle far behind him, Buddy is again drawn into battle with the creatures when they kidnap his young son. Buddy soon learns the Camazotz are as vindictive as they are vicious.

From the Brazilian jungle to the flat Colorado corn fields, Buddy must find the strength and the will to fight. To stop the evil, he must put his trust in strangers and be prepared to make the ultimate sacrifice.

Can he save the world and still save himself?

Available on Amazon in paperback or Kindle edition.